JED STARLIGHT REACHED FOR
THE GREEN RIVER KNIFE

Dimly he could make out a man seated on a packing crate near the front window, a rifle stacked against it, and whoever was sitting there was sucking away at a quart bottle of whiskey. When the bottle found his lips again, Starlight crept forward. His left hand grabbed a hunk of greasy hair while his right brought the cutting edge of the blade around to settle against the man's throat.

"Easy, or I'll open you from ear to ear! Who sent you here?"

"Nobody!" the man blurted out.

"I'll ask one more time," Starlight said coldly, his knife drawing blood.

"Please . . . he'll kill me if I tell you!"

The blade cut deeper. "You're a dead man if you don't!"

WIND RIVER KILL

ROBERT KAMMEN

ZEBRA BOOKS
KENSINGTON PUBLISHING CORP.

ZEBRA BOOKS

are published by

Kensington Publishing Corp.
475 Park Avenue South
New York, NY 10016

Second printing: February, 1990

Printed in the United States of America

1

It appeared to be just a scarecrow dangling from a high limb of the oak tree until you got close enough in the dim light of early morning to see the blackened face with one side almost gouged out where the magpies had been picking at it. The eyes were gone too, and there was no smell; so Jedekiah Starlight knew the rustler had been hanging there for some time. These were dangerous times in Wyoming, the rustler having been left there as a warning to others. Starlight was the only one who so much as glanced at the dead man, because the eyes of the other Slash L hands were fixed on the last rise that lay between them and the lures of Rawlins. They rode eagerly, angling in a ragged line across a shadow-strewn meadow toward the stagecoach road. Sunlight shone golden through the upper reaches of the oak tree standing along a nameless creek, struck the eastern flanks of the Sierra Madres. It had rained during the night, and the loping horses were throwing up clods of turf, the only other sounds the creaking of leather or the snort of a horse.

Clattering onto the road, they followed it to the top

of the rise where they drew up to breathe their horses while gazing appreciatively at Rawlins, some three miles away, awakening to the promise of another hot summer day. The town was spread tidily along the Union Pacific's westward running tracks, with its newer buildings scattered carelessly about like the fringes of a buckskin coat. About a month ago word had come out to the ranch that a political debate was to be held at Rawlins, between the two candidates for governor. Generally these were week-long affairs featuring a parade and other festivities. It would provide a chance to do some rawhiding, and maybe rehash this newfangled idea called Statehood with old friends.

Half of the sun still lay beneath the horizon, but the half that had cleared caused the men to squint away from its harsh orange glare. The expectant banter of hands who hadn't been to town since early spring got to the horses, and they stirred restlessly, wheeling and backing under the bridles or side-stepping nervously.

"Sure seems strange to be a-calling Wyoming a state."

The ramrod, Gar Lamont, said dryly, "Don't matter none to them gals in town what they call this here territory, just so's we've got some hard cash." Swinging his horse sideways, he looked back at Jedekiah Starlight. Lamont was big and heavy, with a pockmarked face; a man who had few friends, and who enjoyed picking on those he considered weaklings. "Ain't that right, kid?" There was an edge to his words, and he grinned derisively when he received no response from Starlight. "Let's ride!" Viciously Lamont dug his spurs into the flanks of his bronc, and it bucked some before breaking out into a gallop, and being followed by the others.

"Every one can master a grief but he that has it."

6

Jedekiah Starlight managed to hold back his prancing horse as he gazed quizzically at a somber and taciturn Mel Longstreet.

"You, Starlight, are a mystery," Longstreet went on, as he brought his grulla to a walk and Starlight moved alongside. Mel Longstreet was a distant cousin of the Southern general of the same name, though he'd kept this to himself. He hadn't believed in the Southern cause, nor did he care much for damnfool Yankees, so at the outbreak of hostilities between the states Longstreet had headed west. He'd been an actor, performing chiefly in large Southern cities, but before the war there'd been a small role at Ford's Theatre in Washington. Though the passage of well over twenty years had dimmed his recollections of Southern life, he still had an intimate knowledge of Shakespeare, and silently quoted from *Cymbeline:* "Golden lads and girls all must, As chimney-sweepers, come to dust." The Longstreets were dark and brooding men, and firm in their minds was a distrust of fair-haired men like Jed Starlight.

Longstreet's dark, lidded eyes went to the kid's sun-dappled profile. He figured Jed Starlight to be around nineteen. Long and loose, with coppery down on his upper lip, blond hair cut mountain fashion, and sort of torquoise-tinted eyes. He knew the kid could handle the .44 Colt percussion tied down at his left hip, but there was considerable difference between killing a rattler and facing someone who'd be shooting back. After spending a long winter with Jed Starlight out at the line camp, there'd come a grudging respect, although the kid had never opened up to him. Some of the mystery of Jed Starlight was due to the possibles he carried in his war bag — beaded moccasins, a fringed doeskin suit, and what Longstreet figured was a Shoshone amulet—along with a Green River knife the kid had snugged up against his right kidney. And Jed Starlight had an uncanny way of heading out alone and coming back with elk or deer meat, this in a trackless land of high peaks and deep ravines and endless timber. Back at the line shack the kid would sit Injun fashion for long periods of time while gazing trancelike at the fireplace or out a window, and though Longstreet had respected these eerie moments of silent reverie, in the eyes of Jed Starlight he'd detected a deep inner pain.

Jed Starlight said quietly, "You know who you are, Mel."

"That's debatable." Though Mel Longstreet told himself he'd left home and family behind because he hadn't believed in what Southerners were fighting for, sometimes he questioned his manhood. Could be he'd been a coward. But what difference did it make now, some twenty years later and older.

"I'm just looking to find out who I am, is all," and saying that, Jed Starlight touched spurs to his horse, and both riders silently cantered past the outlying buildings of Rawlins.

Off to the southwest the moon hung, like a day star, over the mountains as they rode along a main street adorned with fancy banners stretched overhead and red, white, and blue bunting or flags decorating their false fronts business places. There was also a platform located in a vacant lot, but with its front sticking out onto the street, and on it were a rostrum and several hard-backed chairs, the rostrum having what Longstreet decided was the new seal of the state of Wyoming affixed to its front. Across the platform's high backdrop a sign proclaimed that today at high noon the people's choice for governor, Keno Lane, would

8

debate Theopolis J. Gatchell, the candidate favored by the Republicans. Those horses tied along the street were switching their tails at fat blue flies that had been driven out of their night dwelling places as the day warmed up. Farther along the street they passed the gaudy tents of a traveling side show, and then Longstreet swung his horse toward a ramshackle building that was set off by itself.

The legend on the faded sign over the grimy front window read Soo Ling Laundry, and when the kid cast Longstreet a dubious glance, his companion responded in an actor's voice.

"When I was at home I was in a better place; but travelers must be content. I reckon this'll be the only lodging place left in town."

"Reckon so," was Starlight's uncertain reply.

"Soo Ling's an old friend." Longstreet headed around to the back of the building, to a small stable beside which they slid to the ground. Unsaddling their horses, they led them inside and tied them next to a gelding standing listlessly in a large stall. They then went outside to find a short, plump Chinaman smiling at them from the back of the laundry.

"Ah ... Longstreet, you are here again."

"My comrade and I desire the pleasure of your company, Soo Ling."

"You are most welcome."

"This here's Jed Starlight."

Nodding politely at the kid, Soo Ling turned on slippered feet and pushed through the screen door, the others trailing behind. The kitchen was large, Jed Starlight saw, with a large black range squatting against the south wall, and something was stewing in a blue enamel pot, the tangy scent of it teasing his nostrils. Various cooking utensils hung from wall and ceiling hooks, barely illuminated by the daylight that filtered in through the flour-sack curtains covering the three small windows, and the beads of light that seeped through chinks in the log walls. A few flies buzzed around the loaf of bread that sat on the round oaken table, at which Mel Longstreet settled down as the Chinaman went to a cupboard and brought back a couple of tin cups before motioning a tentative Jed Starlight to sit down. The eyes of the kid were fixed uneasily on the small figurine of Buddha, which was smiling back at him.

As the kid reached to take off his hat, there was a sharp squealing noise; then the beaded curtain covering the doorway to the laundry exploded into motion. His left hand curled toward the butt of his holstered gun as a couple of piglets burst into the kitchen to nose around the legs of the strangers.

The Chinaman started to laugh, and Longstreet said through a rare smile, "What's Chinese food without pork?"

Uneasily Jed Starlight eased back down to the table. The long ride in from the ranch had parched him, and he craved a drink of spring water; but when the Chinaman handed him a cup, he had no choice but to sip scalding hot coffee. Thick as blackstrap molasses, it slid down his throat, making his eyes water. He stared uneasily at the cracked porcelain bowl that Soo Ling set before him on the table.

"Right tasty," said Longstreet, as he dug a large spoon into his own bowl.

After a few tentative spoonfuls the kid discovered that he was devouring some of the best vittles he'd had in a long time, and when Longstreet asked for seconds, so did he. When they'd finished eating, the Chinaman brought over a bottle of whiskey and sat down, but

Starlight told the others that he wanted to look the town over. Longstreet's rejoinder that he watch out for tainted women came to him as he stepped outside.

He struck out along the main street. In passing, he noticed activity around the side show, the largest tent having a wide banner stretched before it with the legend WORLD CHAMPION IRISH JACK O'HARA CHALLENGES ALL swirling in foot-high gilt letters. A large painting in a wooden frame was set before the tent. It showed the champion in a boxer's pose, an Adonis with wavy black hair, handlebar mustache, and bronzed torso. Alongside another tent, an unkempt paint horse stood nibbling at what grass it could reach, while through the open flap Starlight could see an Indian, a Sioux judging by the bleached eagle-feather headdress hanging from a tent pole, sleeping on a blanket that needed washing, the big toe of one foot poking through a hole in his shabby moccasin. Some of the allure of side shows left him.

Ambling along the boardwalk, he studied the faces of those he passed, a habit with him whenever he arrived in a new town. The way he'd been abandoned told him he wasn't an orphan, but that had happened when he was going on five, according to the mountain man who'd found and raised him. It wasn't revenge he was seeking from those who'd discarded him; he just needed to know who he was. Once he'd checked out this town, he had it in mind to move on again, maybe follow the railroad eastward and continue his search at those other towns strung out along it.

Up ahead, one of the hands he'd ridden into town with swung through batwings and went the opposite way without noticing Starlight, who resisted the impulse to call out. The kid considered himself a loner, and it was his habit not to speak unless spoken to.

Maybe it was because of this that the ramrod, Lamont, had it in for him. But then again, Gar Lamont liked to bully some of the other hands too. He came to the saloon the Slash L hand had just left, and glanced through a window, and then drew up short when he noticed a large man as blond as he was seated at a poker table. But after a few moments of wondering scrutiny, Jed Starlight felt that the gambler wasn't of his blood and wouldn't know of what had happened before. The kid moved on.

His recollections of that early life were sketchy at best — a dark-haired woman smelling of prairie flowers, two children, and a man picking at a stringed instrument while singing to Jed in a deep baritone voice. Sometimes when the wind moaned through the mountains he again heard that voice raised in song. Though he couldn't recall its name, there was one special song ... the words came muted now through his lips. "... when my true love was young and fair ..." He remembered, also, that the dark-haired woman and the man he believed was his father had gotten into a violent argument over that song, the woman insisting that his father never sing it again. And the big man never had, at least in Starlight's remembrance. On the night of the Sioux raiding party, his father had been away, but the kid would never forget the horror of what had happened. It could be that the dark-haired woman and the other children had been killed, though somehow he felt that they were still alive.

The street drummed hard under his boots when he stepped down from the boardwalk onto it, and after waiting for a lumber wagon to rumble by, he crossed to the other side, where the open door of a grocery store drew him inside. He paid a penny for a shiny red apple. Outside again, he chewed at the apple while strolling

12

toward the Frontier Hotel with its double-decker porch. It was a spacious three-story building, painted white, and as it was close onto mid-morning, the street was getting crowded and the benches in front of the hotel were full. He leaned against a support post and studied those moving past him. Upstreet he noticed some Slash L horses tied to the hitching post in front of the Bullhead Saloon, among them the ramrod's big black. Gar Lamont sure likes his whiskey, Jed thought. A passing woman, whose low-cut gown revealed her bosom, threw Starlight a come-hither smile, and blood tingled his cheeks before she moved on again.

"Here she comes!" someone called out, and Jed Starlight half-turned to see a carriage escorted by a half-dozen horsemen coming down the middle of main street. The carriage had a canvas top and side curtains, and when the driver swung his matched team of bays toward the hotel, the kid noticed the fancy L between the two wreaths on the near door. Those seated on the benches rose as the driver, a cowhand judging from his clothes, reined up. From the way the riders sat warily in their saddles, their dusters opened so that their holstered guns weren't covered, Starlight figured they were hired guns.

The one of the far end looked vaguely familiar. His beard was speckled and one of his eyes squinted against the sun, while the other was larger and sort of bulged out of its socket. "A glass eye," Starlight murmured wonderingly. There was a jagged scar, the skin in it a dullish pink, running across the lower portion of the eye socket and over to the hairline. In the kid's wanderings since leaving the mountains he'd been in a lot of towns, and it could have been in one of these that he'd seen the hired gun or on some wanted poster. But the notion struck him that it could have been even earlier. Then he set that thought aside as a young woman hopped down from the carriage.

Jed Starlight stopped chewing on the mouthful of apple, and stared, transfixed, at the silky raven hair spilling to the woman's tiny waist, the long blue satin dress clinging to her full-bodied figure. The woman smiled at those gathered under the porch; then her wide hazel eyes, golden flecks dancing in them, swung over to where the kid was standing. He seemed to become weak limbed under the spell of those eyes, and his heart pounded loudly against his rib cage. When another woman emerged from the carriage to step between Starlight and the younger woman, it was as if a cloud or a shadow had passed between them.

The other woman wore a satin cape thrown over her full-length dress and a dark blue bonnet with a veil that covered her face. And she had dark hair, the kid noticed. Suddenly she raised her veil to stare hard at Starlight, and he recoiled from the hatred he saw blazing out of her eyes. He knew that women of substance didn't want their daughters messing around with lowly cowhands, but hatred such as she was throwing at him wasn't natural—it had a deeper root. The woman spun to throw a protective arm around the younger woman's shoulders, and together they hurried into the hotel. Along with that piercing look of hatred, Jed Starlight had seen something else flashing out of that woman's eyes. Could it be fear? he wondered. Without a shred of doubt, he knew he'd see that woman again.

As Jed Starlight glanced around, he noticed the respectful way the men had stood to remove their hats, and wanting to find out who these women were, he stepped over to a bench. "Pardon me, sir, but could you tell me who owns that carriage?"

Through a chuckle the man said, "Sonny, you mean to tell me you come here for this political debate and you don't know who that is? Why, her picture's been in all the papers. Sonny, that just happens to be Etta Montclair Lane, wife of our esteemed Senator Keno Lane . . . who's gonna defeat that damned Republican candidate. You yonkers sure don't know nothing about politics . . ."

Mumbling his thanks, Jed Starlight swung away and headed downstreet, his mind clouded by what had just happened. During his lonely sojourns in search of his past he'd seen many comely young women, and some willing to know him better, but the raven-haired woman outshone them all. Well, he mused, there's no sense setting my sights on her.

When he came to the marshal's office, his pace slowed. The history of Rawlins and other Western towns was of hardships suffered at the hands of renegades and Indians. The marshal could probably narrate to him stories of others who'd been abducted or killed. With a tug at his hat he hurried on. He passed the remainder of the morning wandering along the main street and the narrower side streets. On one of these he found himself by some holding pens strung along the railroad tracks; in the next, he watched a train disgorge a few passengers at the depot before it headed west again. It was almost noon when he returned to main street to find that a crowd had congregated around the stand where the debate was to be held. As he headed that way, Mel Longstreet called to him.

Crossing the street, Jed fell into step with Longstreet, who asked, "You getting hungry?"

"Later, maybe."

"From that look in your eye I reckon you'll be cutting your ties with the ranch."

"Hankering to do that, Mel."

Longstreet said sagely, "It's been my experience that if one wants to get someone talking a snifter or two of whiskey has mouth-opening tendencies."

"That a fact?" Starlight grinned.

"It's high time you was weaned, kid." Longstreet waved a hand at a saloon at the end of the block. "Yonder den of iniquity beckons."

"Thought I'd hear what them politicians have to say."

"Only jackasses and the feeble-minded ever pay a politician any heed. This way, kid." Crooking a beckoning finger, Longstreet pushed through the batwings; then Starlight followed him into the saloon.

Jed Starlight wasn't a stranger to liquor, having tried it once or twice, but he found that it didn't suit his style, though a cold beer on a hot day was welcome. Longstreet managed to shoulder a place for them at the crowded bar, and the kid stuck a spurred boot on the foot rest. While they waited for a barkeep to serve them, he watched in the mirror at the back of the bar, what was going on behind him. All of the poker tables were going, as was a monte game. Starlight smiled when he saw one of the women who worked there deftly pick the back pocket of a man who stood in a tight cluster around the piano. "The wages of sin don't come cheap," he murmured.

"Leave the bottle," Longstreet told the barkeep, who scooped up the silver dollar and swung to another customer. Filling their shot glasses, Longstreet downed his and washed the taste away with a sip from the stein of beer before he nudged Starlight's arm. "Mighty tasty, kid." He watched as Starlight emptied the glass and threw him a clear-eyed smile. "Reckon you've been weaned already."

"Some," Jed admitted.

"Where you figure on heading?"

"East, maybe."

"You owe me."

"How's that, Mel?"

Longstreet refilled their glasses. He fished out a cheroot and bit the end away. "I put up with you one long winter out at that line camp, kid. You know, you ain't the best of company at times."

"You had your testy moments too."

"Age has its allowances." Mel scratched a wooden match on the worn bar top, touched flame to the cheroot, and dragged smoke deep into his lungs. "For just being a run-of-the-mill cowpoke you know too much. Like you've been places most of us ain't."

"There's ain't much to tell."

"I'm listening, kid."

While forming his thoughts Starlight picked up his shot glass and studied the amber contents in it before he said quietly, "My life's a story you've probably heard before." Then, as best he could, he began the telling of how he was found and raised by mountain man Cree Bonner; and of Bonner's desire that he leave the mountains when the time was ripe, and find the source of his roots. "So far I haven't had much luck, Mel."

"Having roots is important. You know, kid, I've got this feeling that if you keep looking there'll be trouble. Seems to me, though, you ain't got no other choice."

"Am I loco!" It was Gar Lamont's whiskey-slurred voice. "Or is the kid actually drinking some hard stuff?" The batwings were still swinging behind other Slash L hands who'd crowded in after the ramrod.

Lamont shoved his hat back to reveal a receding hairline. The rim had left a reddish groove on his forehead, and the skin above that showed white. The ramrod's eyes were filled with contempt for Jed Starlight, and they were red rimmed from drinking. In the confined space of saloon he looked bulkier than he was, but when he shoved past some bystanders to get to the bar his walk was clumsy. He hadn't bothered to clean up; at least two day's growth of stubble darkened his blunt jawline and trail dust lay in the grooves of his trousers and woolen shirt.

Longstreet cut in. "Lay off, Gar."

"This is between the kid and me," Lamont lashed out. "That is . . . unless you're cutting yourself into the game." He spat tobacco juice down at the sawdust.

"I can handle it," Starlight said quietly, and he turned to face the ramrod. From Cree Bonner he'd learned the rudiments of rough and tumble fighting, but if it came down to bare knuckles he'd have to move quick to have any chance at all. Up in the mountains there'd been one-on-one situations, him against grizzlies or puma, so the kid figured he had the advantage, for despite the ramrod's size and his holstered .45 Colt Peacemaker, the man's reflexes would be slowed by drink and conceit. Strangely enough, he felt no fear, only a dreamy calmness, as if the horror of what had happened to him when he'd been abandoned had plumbed the depths of his fear, leaving him ready for what life could throw at him.

"It comes down to a matter of honor, kid," Lamont said loudly, his words intended for everyone there. "The horror of the Slash L spread — ain't that right, boys?"

"We done drew straws on it," Cooty Blaine put in. He was one of the hands who generally hung out with the ramrod. "And you come up with short straw, Star-light."

"Yup," said Lamont through a cocky smile. "No world champion boxer's gonna come into our stompin' grounds and not be challenged. It boils down to this, kid. Either you fight Irish Jack O'Hara or I'll have to do it. But if you chicken out, kid, it's my intention to pile and hammer you."

Mel Longstreet said, "Jed won't have a chance against that fighter, Lamont, and you know it. Dammit, this has gone far—"

"I'll do it," Starlight said firmly.

The ramrod's eyes flared open in surprise, but you could see he was disappointed in what the kid had said by the way he ran the back of his hand across his mouth to wipe away a trickle of tobacco juice. Angrily he settled his hat back over his forehead.

"You sure about this?"

Jed glanced at Longstreet. "Got no other choice."

"Lamont's three sheets to the wind. Maybe you'd have a better chance with him."

"Look at it this way, Mel, how many men get the chance to challenge a world champion?"

"Kid, you've been bucked off of too many broncs," Longstreet declared sorrowfully.

"Well, Gar," said one of the hands, "I'll buy this round before we head out for that side show."

"Buy, hell!" Lamont retorted sullenly. "Let's head over to that three-ringed circus before the kid chickens out. A double eagle says he don't last over fifteen seconds."

"Done!" piped up a gambler, as he hopped up from his chair and accosted the ramrod. He threw Starlight an appraising glance. "On the other hand, let's make it double that."

19

"Damned right!" Gar Lamont said. Then he shoved his way clear to the door and went outside.

The other Slash L hands followed in a bunch, along with the gamblers, and some of the women, and the barkeeps. As the kid followed Longstreet out onto the street, Longstreet said wryly, "A hanging or the sight of blood sure brings out the worst in people."

By the time they reached the side show, others had heard about what was to happen and had hurried over to gather around the tent displaying the picture of the world champion. The ramrod was talking to a fat man with muttonchops that tickled his ears. This stranger wore a black hat like preachers wear and a black frock coat. A golden watch chain ran across his ample belly. In a sonorous voice he introduced himself as Colonel F. J. Avalon, out of Boston, and announced that tickets would be four bits a head, which brought a murmur of dissent from the crowd. His false teeth clicked and moved around in his mouth when he talked, but the eyes below the thick black brows were shrewd.

"Now, folks, surely you don't expect to get in for nothing to see the world champion." Sweeping off his hat, he pointed it at the framed picture. "Irish Jack O'Hara kayoed Kid Galadan in five — won a hard-earned decision over Sullivan himself."

"We ain't a damned bit interested in his pedigree," Gar Lamont said sourly. "We've got ourselves a challenger."

"In that case," said Avalon, "just pay your entrance fee to Red Cloud over there while I roust the champion." As he hurried away, the Indian Jed Starlight had seen sleeping in one of the tents was solemnly taking coin from those wanting to see the fight.

The kid could feel curious eyes upon him as he went with Mel Longstreet up to the ring around which long benches had been placed. On the walk over from the saloon, it had occurred to him that he could simply ride out of town, because he wasn't overly upset about Gar Lamont's bullying ways. Still, if the ramrod had started a ruckus, the kid knew that only one man would have walked away from it.

"You'd best take off your boots, and maybe shuck your shirt," said Longstreet. "Loosen up some."

"How're you betting?"

"I'm saving what coin I've got for your doctor. Dammit, kid, you're playing right into Lamont's hands." Starlight's hat was handed to him, and then his shirt; and Mel Longstreet gazed appraisingly at the younger man's lithe but muscular torso, and at the birthmark shaped like the wings of an eagle just below his breastbone. The birthmark was about the size of a double eagle, and when the kid flexed his arms to loosen his muscles, that dark purplish mark seemed too come alive, its outer tips fluttering winglike as if it wanted to soar away to the mountains. Longstreet had never seen the likes of that birthmark before, but the appearance of the world champion drew his attention across the ring.

This was no godlike Adonis. Irish Jack O'Hara was about the largest man Jed Starlight had ever seen, and maybe one who'd been mauled by a crazed grizzly, for scar tissue lay thick around deep set eyes that blazed with contempt. The boxer's face looked like he used sandpaper to toughen his skin, and there were a few more scars around his wide mouth, while one ear was misshapen. But there was no hair on his huge chest or gleaming head, and despite the world champion's menacing appearance, a little flab showed at his midsection. A glimmer of hope came to the kid as Avalon

21

tossed a pair of boxing gloves to him. The ring groaned and heaved when Irish Jack O'Hara swung up into it, the ropes hemming it in twanging like guy wires, and Starlight found, as he entered the ring, that the thin padding covering the planking would be of little use if he was knocked down.

"You ever have gloves on before?"

"Nope."

Longstreet groaned. Hurriedly he tightened the lacings as Colonel Avalon moved around the ring to place bets with the handful of betters wagering against the champion. When the kid glanced around he was surprised to discover that the tent was jammed. He shut the noise from his mind and looked at his opponent, who was glowering at him from the opposite corner.

"You're going down!" the champion snarled.

Smiling with his eyes, the kid said quietly, "You know, Mel, I do believe Irish Jack O'Hara's taken a liking to me."

Again Longstreet groaned. "Guess I don't have to worry none about him giving you any brain damage, kid. That seems to be something you've already got. Just stay away from him!"

"Ladies and gentlemen!" shouted Colonel F. J. Avalon through clicking false teeth. "The conditions of this bout are as follows. If the challenger lasts three rounds"—a wave of derisive laughter and catcalls rose and then fell—"with the world champion, I will personally give this gallant young man here a double eagle piece. This bout will be fought under the Marquis of Queensberry rules. The timekeeper is my loyal friend, Red Cloud. And the referee is from your fair city of Rawlins . . . ah, yes . . . Abe Muldoon, who barkeeps at the Bullhead Saloon."

The colonel struggled through the ropes, the bell

22

sounded, and World Champion Irish Jack O'Hara bounded up from his stool and across the ring toward the kid. A prod in the back from Longstreet brought Jed Starlight to his feet. He raised his gloves in what he considered a defensive position and managed to side-step to evade a looping right thrown by O'Hara. Close in like this, the kid realized his adversary was even larger than mountain man Cree Bonner, who generally made most men back down. Back-pedaling along the ropes, he found that the ring wasn't as big as it appeared from the outside, and that keeping away from O'Hara would be a sizable chore.

The world champion wheeled around and flexed his arms as he again came snarling toward the kid. Mouthing an obscenity, O'Hara feinted with a left and threw a cocked right, the blow catching Starlight alongside the head. O'Hara smiled through gapped teeth when his opponent staggered backward against the ropes.

"Punk, you're going down. . . ." he snarled.

He came in with a straight left, only to miss as the kid spun away along the ropes, provoking more curses from the champion.

Though it had been a glancing blow, the kid knew that if Irish Jack O'Hara hit him flush the fight would be over, for the pain of that blow still rode with him. He felt as though his right ear had been ripped off.

The way of grizzlies was to come at a man full bore, and Starlight had this in mind as he pivoted on stockinged feet and came at the world champion, feinting first with a left hook, then a right, and when Irish Jack O'Hara stopped to stare in puzzled wonder at this sudden display of foolish courage, he lashed out with his right foot and kicked O'Hara in the crotch. The kid reasoned that up in the mountains no critter would have any use for the Marquis of Queensberry rules.

As the world champion doubled up in pain, Gar Lamont and others shouted, "Foul!"

At the frantic tolling of the bell, the referee pulled the kid away from the stricken champion while an irate Colonel F. J. Avalon heaved himself through the ropes. Spectators were shouting that the fight should resume.

"Foul, dammit, the fight's over!" Avalon cried. And even as Starlight was being led to his corner by the referee, an enraged Irish Jack O'Hara was struggling to his feet. Staggering across the ring, he knocked the referee through the ropes and began to hammer at Jed Starlight from behind. The first blow slammed the kid against the ring post, stunning him. He tried to turn to defend himself, but the jolting blows thrown by O'Hara found their mark and he fell to the canvas.

Mel Longstreet clambered into the ring. Drawing his revolver, he jammed the barrel into O'Hara's midriff. "You kick the kid once more and you're a dead man!"

Snarling, the world champion drew away, and he was still mumbling curses when Colonel Avalon led him out of the ring.

When Jed Starlight regained consciousness it was to find Mel Longstreet bending over him, with the Chinaman hovering in the background. Afternoon sunlight came through the bedroom window.

"Where am I?"

"At Soo Ling's, kid. You sure took some hard blows. But the doctor feels there ain't any brain damage; no more'n you've already got. That was a stupid move, kicking the world champion in his privates." Despite his anger, Longstreet grinned and added, "It sure got O'Hara's attention, though."

"Seems to me," Starlight said, wincing, "the ramrod bet that I wouldn't last over fifteen seconds."

"Gar Lamont ain't too sharp when it comes to gambling. Look, kid, just lay there and take it easy. I'm hankering for some gambling and a woman or two. See you later."

Jed Starlight drifted off to sleep, to dream of prize fighters and grizzlies, and the mountains. In his dreamworld, too, was the raven-haired woman he'd seen getting out of that carriage and being taken away by that other woman . . . and a kid searching for her and his shadowy past. When he awoke, the bedroom was cloaked in darkness. He felt refreshed and though the dizziness was gone, there was a slight twinge in his ribs when he eased out of bed. Out in the kitchen, he washed up, and in the broken shard of mirror hanging above the sink, he surveyed the damage done to his face. "You'll live," he told himself. Then he winked at the Buddha, donned his hat, and went out the back door.

He'd never seen fireworks before, and the sight of multicolored lights exploding into falling patterns over the northern outskirts of Rawlins held him on the back porch. He could hear the sounds, see the lights of the main street. There was an off-chance that he might run into that young woman, but at the moment he wasn't in the mood to seek her out. After saddling his horse, he found the lane that would take him to the creek he'd seen when coming into town. The heat of day hung, sultry, in the air, and he held his bronc at a canter. Gingerly he pressed probing fingers against his rib cage, and was relieved to find that he didn't have any cracked ribs.

When some aspens loomed up against the horizon, he left the lane and rode over to the creek, followed it until Rawlins had fallen behind screening brush and trees. Coming to a fallen cottonwood extending into the water, he dismounted and sat down on it. Once in a while the moon would peek out from behind scattered clouds drifting to the southeast, gently lower moonbeams across the dark-gleaming waters, but the kid's thoughts weren't on the works of nature. The fight had slipped from his mind too, for it had been merely a diversion. He felt no rancor toward Irish Jack O'Hara, although he'd welcome another encounter with the ramrod, Lamont.

"Etta Montclair Lane?" he said thoughtfully. The woman's strange behavior that morning still puzzled him. Once she'd been beautiful, but in the quick glance he'd had she'd showed signs of aging. Hatred would do that to a person, he knew. The trick was to let go, forgive others; Cree Bonner had preached it to him enough times. But this Etta Lane woman seemed to be the kind of person who couldn't forget nor forgive, if he'd read her right. He'd met a few others like that, mostly gunslingers or those down on their luck, and he'd given these people a wide berth. Still, it was strange that a woman of wealth and breeding would carry on like this.

Then again, the other woman had seemed like a breath of spring air when she'd stepped out of that carriage. She'd been vibrant, alive with a radiance that outshone the sun's even. His blood churned faster as he recalled those dancing hazel eyes beaming into his. She was a once-in-a-lifetime woman, one out of the reach of an ordinary cowpoke.

"Besides, you ain't got any roots, Starlight," he reminded himself. But he knew that his emotions had been stirred by that young woman. Anyway, no sense mooning over her, for it was his notion to vamoose from this town come sunup. He'd miss Mel Longstreet's cutting humor, though.

Climbing into the saddle, he went farther along the creek and finally cut away from it to ride out onto the prairie, where the black outline of the mountains held his gaze, his longing for them bringing back bitter memories. When he came to the stagecoach road, he followed it back to Rawlins.

He bypassed the main street to ride along the narrow side street lined with houses. Lilac bushes that had been trimmed into shape grew along in front of them, but he could see by moonlight that brown withered grass passed for what lawn there was. Once in a while he'd see a stable behind a house, along with a row of outhouses, and there were some clotheslines, too. Lights beamed from windows, and he'd catch an occasional glimpse of someone moving about inside or seated. Rawlins had the feel of domesticity to it, which, according to Cree Bonner, was worse than getting a social disease; and at the moment Starlight shared the mountain man's sentiments. Why, he told himself, a man could sicken and die within a week of settling into a place like this. Or, at the very least, get the seven-year itch. He smiled at the notion, and as if divining the kid's thoughts, the bronc tossed its head back to nibble at an itch on its shoulder.

When Starlight had cleared the houses, he brought his bronc, at a walk, past a blacksmith shop shuttered for the night before he saw the small stable behind Soo Ling's laundry. He came alert when he spotted the five horses ground-hitched behind the building, and he reined up, trying to stab through the darkness to see their riders. Without warning, gunfire came from the

27

front of the stable, and Jed Starlight vaulted out of the saddle as five men ran toward the horses. Upon spotting Starlight, they opened fire. Ducking behind a nearby tree, he fired back, but sprawled to the ground when slugs from their weapons riddled the trunk. As his assailants swung aboard their horses and pulled away from the stable, Starlight emptied his revolver, and saw one of the riders slump in his saddle before all of them vanished around another building. Pushing up from the ground, he ran around the stable and found Longstreet sprawled out on the back porch.

"Mel!" he shouted.

Kneeling down, he grimaced at the blood staining Longstreet's woolen shirt, but though it was thready, he found a pulse. He dragged Longstreet away from flames starting to flicker out of a window. "The Chinaman!" Reasoning that Soo Ling could still be inside, he ran onto the back porch and shouldered through the back door, his momentum carrying him into the kitchen. One sickening glance at what the kitchen contained told him what had happened here. Soo Ling lay face up on the table, blood trickling from the slit in his throat to mingle with the blood of the piglets lying dead on the floor. A flaming beam crashed down, driving Jed outside, where he found others converging on the laundry.

He stood over the fallen Longstreet, stunned by what had happened. As far as he knew, Mel Longstreet didn't have any enemies, at least none around these parts. And who'd want to kill Soo Ling? Gar Lamont was a bully, but Starlight doubted that the man's wayward ways extended to murder. But what was it that Longstreet had said? That delving into Jed Starlight's past could bring trouble.

"You all right, kid?"

"Yeah, yeah," he mumbled to one of the Slash L hands.

The cowhand bent over Longstreet, shouted to the others, "We'd best get him to a sawbones before he cashes in his chips. Lend a hand here!"

Jed Starlight stumbled away from the burning building, headed in the general direction of where he'd left his horse. He knew with a deep feeling of dread that what had happened here had been because of him. And he also knew that in order to find out who was behind this he'd have to travel the backtrail into the time when the mountain man had found him, go back to that night of terror.

2

Long after a more cautious man would have bedded down for the night, Cree Bonner kept pressing deeper into the Wind River Basin. This was Indian country, Crow and some Arapaho, but he doubted that any hostiles would be on the prowl, though he wouldn't bet his pack horse against it, which was why he cast an occasional eye on his backtrail.

He'd never seen the sky so filled with stars, some shooting, and a whole black dome full of others dazzling to the old mountain man's eyes. There was the wide band of Milky Way overhead, with the North Star holding steady over his right shoulder as he rode. By the silvery cast of starlight, mesquite and sagebrush were revealed to him, cottonwoods cupping the starlight in their leaves, mesas shimmering low along the horizon, and the mountains where he was headed, bending darkly away.

"Damned near bright as day," he mumbled in Shoshone, then spit down at the clayey red soil shining dully on the south bank of the Wind River.

A week behind Cree Bonner were the settlements. Civilization had waggled an enticing finger at him and he'd flicked a scorning one back. He was still unsettled over the price he'd gotten for his furs. "That trader was worse than a back-stabbing Crow," he grumbled angrily. Though whiskey and a few loose women had worn off the raw edges of winter, he rode with the stench of the settlements still in his nostrils and a feeling that maybe one of the women had presented him with the clap, or worse. The townsmen had worn frock coats and string ties, and had moved about as though rheumatism were stiffening up their joints. None of them had had an honest face, except for that preacher fellow who'd had a pendulous lower lip like a woman and who'd tried to cast the devils out of Cree Bonner once he'd found out about Teal Eyes, Bonner's Shoshone squaw.

"Should have gelded that heathen." Hawking to clear his throat, Cree spat riverward.

There was in Bonner a reckless nature, which he'd tamed a little after all his years in the mountains, but there was a wide difference between that and being careless, which no man had ever accused him of and lived. His cayuse, a Cherokee pony, a piebald with a great profusion of mane and tail, had been acting skittish ever since they'd cut down toward the river. Cree Bonner knew that something was wrong, and it rankled him that he couldn't put his finger on it.

Approaching a stretch of river where white water ran through a gorge, Bonner urged his cayuse up the bank and away from the river until he drew up in a copse of birch trees. Plucking a leaf, he chewed on it to draw out the moisture as he let his bodily senses dictate his next move. Only two things would stir up the cayuse, Indians or a grizzly, neither of which he wanted to encounter under any circumstances. The moon stole out from behind the Owl Creek range and drifted about a hand's length to the southwest before he heard the muted yowling of a timber wolf . . . a couple more joined in, and the night became lonelier.

"Just so's them critters ain't after us," he muttered. "And now we've gotta travel under moonlight too." He urged the cayuse and pack horse into a rock-strewn meadow. Once he was in the open, starlight gleamed off the metal parts of his Hawken rifle and saddle rigging. A large man, he rode slouched in the saddle, with the rifle cradled in his arm. Gray streaked his full beard and the mane of shaggy brown hair tumbling down from under the fur cap onto his powerful shoulders. Over the fringed buckskins he had a buckskin capote, a loose affair that draped from shoulders to knees, and hanging around his neck was a Shoshone amulet. As he rode, Bonner debated over whether or not he should hole up, knowing that a few miles ahead the Wind River was guarded by high bluffs, a choice spot for an ambush. But the thought of passing through here in the morning kept him in the saddle. There was still about a week's journey before him, and once he got out of the basin and through Togwotee Pass things would set easier in his mind. Then the skin at the base of his skull crawled a little when the yowling of that wolf pack came louder, closer. "Could be some stoved-up elk they're after." The cayuse sidestepped, and he patted its shoulder to quiet it down.

Once the meadow had fallen behind, Cree Bonner cleared another stand of trees to find himself coming on the river again, where it flowed through a level stretch of ground but with higher elevations to either side. This was Indian country, pure and simple. Bonner's one original notion had been to trap beaver, and he'd had some good seasons, along with the annual rendezvous at Pierre's Hole, until they'd petered out. He could always go live with Teal Eye's people, become a full-fledged squawman. But damned if he'd let civilization get its hooks into him again. Let them who was plow minded have that mule crap.

The banks of the Wind River lowered until it seemed its sparkling waters were flowing through a meadow strewn with mountain flowers, and then the nearby snarl of a timber wolf brought Cree Bonner's cayuse into frightened bucking as it tried to throw its rider. "Whoa, dammit!" he cried out, taking a firmer grip on his rifle while fighting to stay in the saddle. "Should have sold you to the Crows when I had the chance." Only after he'd managed to settle the cayuse down did he see the elusive forms of several timber wolves move out of the screening brush and close on the river from both sides. At this point the Wind River was no more than thirty yards in width, and there was a sandy stretch of shoreline on its northern side, where the wolves seemed to be heading.

"Wal, I'll be?" From where Cree Bonner sat atop his horse he made out some living thing staked down on the bank opposite, something that gleamed stark white in the starlight and then cried out, to the mountain man's amazement.

Cree Bonner exclaimed: "It's . . . a . . . a child." One of the wolves darted in, and without thinking or seeming to aim Bonner brought the rifle to his shoulder and fired. The wolf spun around in midair and toppled over.

"Wagh!" he yelled, as he dug his moccasins into the flanks of the cayuse, and at a gallop, both of his horses splashed into the river and swam to the far bank. The sudden appearance of the mountain man drove the wolf pack back and it melted into the edges of the brush, but he could still see their yellow-gleaming eyes. Vaulting out of the saddle, he reloaded the Hawken rifle, an instinctive move. *A mangeur de lard*, one of those not accustomed to the way of it out here, would probably go see what he'd found without reloading, and maybe pay the price for his carelessness.

In all the years Bonner had been roaming around the mountains he'd seen some strange sights, been involved in a lot of bloodletting, seen others like him savaged by Indians, but what he was staring at now stunned his imagination.

Staked out naked at his feet was a man child, possibly of the tender age of five, and with a hunk of raw venison dripping blood onto its small rib cage. The boy's skin was broken open and bleeding where leather thongs had cut into wrists and ankles, and the eyes that stared into Bonner's were of a peculiar blue color, not containing fear but a sharp interest in what was happening. Bonner was of the mind that he'd never seen a blonder mop of hair on any white child. Unsheathing his Green River knive, he hunkered down, and was taken back when the man child spoke.

"Are you an Injun, too?"

He blinked to hide his surprise. "Wal now, I ain't." He cut the thongs away before picking up the hunk of meat and throwing it in the direction of the circling wolfs. That shot he'd fired might alert any Indians camped in the immediate vicinity, but they weren't the ones who'd done this to the man child. His instincts told him this was white man's work, done by those who had an even crueler nature than the Arapaho. He looked about for sign, came across moccasin tracks and hoofprints made by an unshod horse. It didn't make any sense, someone bringing a man child this far out into the wilderness only to leave him to the wolves.

Could be this same person had heard the shot and might be circling back, or some Indians camped nearby might be checking it out.

He went to the packhorse and tore a piece of cloth from the printed material he'd bought for Teal Eyes. After dipping it in water, he wiped the blood from the man child's chest, drawling, "Ain't never seen a birthmark the likes of that before; mighty peculiar. Wal, it's too far back to the settlements ... and my Bible training tells me I can't leave you here. You got a name, child?"

"J-Jed ... I think."

Then he realized the man child had gone into shock, and silently he cursed the person who'd done this before he eased the naked form into his arms. Once he was astride the cayuse, he tucked the child under the folds of his capote and headed west along the Wind River.

Approaching the high bluffs through which the river flowed, Bonner crossed to the southern side and rode into heavier stands of virgin timber while following the upward slope of the land to the crest of a rocky bluff. On its summit, a cool breeze reached out for him. Sneaking a peek at the man child, Bonner saw to his satisfaction that he'd fallen asleep. He pulled up and looked down at the river. Patiently he waited while the cayuse nibbled at alpine forget-me-nots sprouting from a crevice in the rock. Nearly twenty minutes passed before movement on the northern side of the river caught his eye, and then horsemen appeared. Crow, he figured, and loping eastward. They'd be riled up when they came to the place where Bonner had found the man child, and he was hoping they'd take after that other horseman.

"It'll serve the murdering bastard right if they catch

35

him," he muttered.

The man child stirred under the capote, shifted his arms to make himself more comfortable, and Bonner eased the cayuse away from the rim of the bluff and to the west as he thought of his squaw.

"Teal Eyes always did want a kid," he said reflectively. "Wal, now she's got one. Though she'll damn well never believe I found this here man child out in the boonies." A sudden grin revealed his bone-white teeth.

Then his teeth snapped together when he felt something warm and kind of moist come trickling onto his lap. Quickly he tossed the capote aside, cupped one large hand under the man child's backside, and held him away. An angry mountain man eyeballed the man child who'd come awake and was gazing curiously back at him.

"I've been shot at! I've been quilled by arrows! Cursed at, called a liar and a no-account squawman! But I ain't never been pissed on before!" Cree Bonner was beside himself with rage at what had happened until he glimpsed a tear falling pearl-like from the man child's left eye.

His anger expelled, he said quietly, "Guess I had no call to explode like that." A sudden smile squinted his eyes, and he held the man child higher so that starlight seemed to halo the blond hair. "Wagh. It was by starlight I found you . . . so Starlight you'll be. Yup, man child, Jed Starlight."

"I'm . . . hungry," the man child cried out as tears came in earnest from his eyes.

Bringing the man child closer to his chest and back into the folds of his capote, Bonner said, "We'll make camp at first light, which ain't too far off."

Six days later Cree Bonner and the man child, Jed Starlight, were moving through high plateau country

36

and coming strong on the Grand Tetons skylined beyond the Snake River. They rode along the river while Bonner studied both sides of it to find out if Indians or other mountain men had passed through during his absence. He had cut down one of his shirts so that it fit Jed Starlight who rode with his legs slung on either side of the cayuse's shoulders, holding the reins. During the week they'd been together, Bonner had asked the man child a few probing questions as to where he came from. But the tender age of Jed Starlight had been a barrier through which no answers except the man child's first name had passed, and Bonner had let it go at that.

They forded the river, where it was eddying around sunken rocks, coming closer to the jagged peaks. Around noon Bonner ducked under the branches of an aspen as he brought the cayuse to the edge of a large lake, scaring a moose that had been feeding in a marshy area off to their right. "This be Jackson Lake . . . and off yonder be chimney smoke. Got myself a snug little cabin back in deep timber," he said. Though the man child had taken some to venison and beef jerky, he'd demanded milk, a commodity unknown to these parts. The kid, he'd found out, gagged on whiskey, while water didn't seem to satisfy his thirst. As he rode on, keeping away from the curving stretch of shoreline, it occurred to Bonner that he just might have to cross the Tetons and buy a cow from Teal Eyes' people, the Shoshone.

About halfway around the lake the mountain man veered away from it, passed through a meadow where beargrass rippled against his legs and then headed into another stand of timber before the cayuse nickered as its hoofs struck a narrow lane running toward a small log cabin. A pinto standing in a pole corral cocked its ears at their arrival and a woman ran out of the cabin. Teal Eyes was tall for a Shoshone woman, the doeskin dress she wore setting off her ample bosom and wide hips. Her jet black hair was braided and hung down her back, in a long plait, and her eyes were the color of ripe olives. She reached for Bonner's hand to grasp it while gazing questioningly up at him.

"Now, woman, I can explain the presence of this man child. Jed Starlight, this be Teal Eyes." Swinging to the ground, he lifted Starlight onto a brawny shoulder, and with the woman coming behind, went into the cabin. "Them vittles shore smell good, woman."

Teal Eyes spoke in Shoshone. "Did you steal the boy?"

"I found him, woman," He rasped out. "He'd been left to die out in Wind River country. Strangest thing I've ever seen, him staked out like that. Shore was unsettling." As she rattled on again in her language, Bonner gave his head a wearying shake and then set the man child on the table. "He craves milk, woman!"

"Milk?" she cried out. "Then bring me a bighorn sheep."

"You've got tits, woman, feed him!"

Spinning past the fireplace, Teal Eyes reached for a knife, and the mountain man, Cree Bonner, bolted outside as the hunting knife thudded into the door closing behind him.

Jed Starlight gazed at the familiar sight of Grand Teton rising slender as a lodge-pole pine, the other jagged peaks of the range strung out to either side. He'd come to know the moods of these mountains, and how melt-off sustained every manner of life in this high plateau country. As the seasons changed, so did

38

these gigantic slabs of rock rising some thirteen thousand feet from the sage flats to glint with subdued hues of gray or blue between patches of snow. Coming onto his fifteenth birthday now, he'd learned from Cree Bonner most of the mysteries of these peaks the Blackfoot called Big Breasts, though Bonner had often told him that he must have been born under a lucky star because of all the learning mistakes he'd made. More often than not, the mountain man would make it clear where Starlight's destiny lay, but the thought of venturing down to the plains didn't set right in his mind. This was his home now.

He stared at Cree Bonner riding ahead of him. They were heading north into Yellowstone country to scout out untrapped streams for beaver. But something seemed to be troubling Bonner. Generally he'd be whistling softly or taking a sizable bite from the plug of chewing tobacco he always carried. Jed had found out that Bonner was pretty much set in his ways, which was one reason the lever-action Winchester was stuck in Starlight's saddle boot while Bonner still relied on that old Hawken.

When Bonner's brown gelding perked up its ears, he swung around and looked back at Starlight, who'd also pulled up, only to have the packhorse bump into the hindquarters of his pinto.

"Something don't smell right," Bonner said tautly. "I feel it in my bones."

Starlight never questioned the aging mountain man's instincts, and now he keened his ears and senses to the swampy land adjoining the Snake River. They were headed due north, having passed Jackson Lake at first light. He scanned what sky he could make out above the trees to see if any birds had taken wing, turned his attention to some terns floating with the current on the river surface, and then Bonner gestured with his hand.

"Cross over, Jed, and scout out the other side."

He swung his horse around a thorny bush and let it and the packhorse pick their way down the bank, their unshod hoofs making a sucking noise upon being pulled out of the thick mud, and once he was across, Starlight unsheathed his rifle to lever a shell into its breech. On this side the bottomland was more sandy and littered with various-sized rocks; he avoided these by riding through a grassy meadow. Now he could sense it too, that others were in the general vicinity. Underbrush forced him farther away from the river and into ponderosas murmuring as a cool mountain breeze drifted through them, their piny scent wafting into Starlight's nostrils. Then he swung toward the river again and came alert when he saw the remains of a campfire, the hoof-prints left by several horses. Without dismounting, he recognized moccasin tracks left by Blackfoot Indians.

"A war party," he murmured grimly. The Blackfoot, he knew, were the most feared of all mountain Indians, warring with other tribes and white men alike. Jed Starlight knew sign as well as he knew his own mind, and what he found here told him that fifteen Blackfeet had camped here last night, had left before sunup and ridden south. He whistled softly. The answering call of a loon came from across the river, and then Cree Bonner appeared and looked about cautiously before crossing over to Starlight.

"I don't like them heading south like this," Bonner said ominously. "Could be they're headed for the cabin. Let's ride, Jed, and hard."

They brought their horses away from the river and into a ground-eating lope that carried them through clutching underbrush and around trees, but in cleared spaces they traveled at a gallop, the fear of what would happen if that raiding party found Teal Eyes keeping their eyes trained southward. After they'd ridden for about an hour, they stopped to let their horses breathe, and to rinse out their mouths with water from their canteens, both of them remaining silent. Jed Starlight had come to love the old mountain man, though it was a different love he felt for Teal Eyes. Bonner called her some hunk of woman, but the kid wasn't certain what that meant yet. Within moments Bonner was on the move again, Starlight a couple of yards behind.

Now they were catching glimpses of Jackson Lake which lay at the base of the Grand Tetons, and then Cree Bonner cursed at the distant crackle of gunfire. He lashed his reins down at the shoulders of the gelding.

Starlight let his horse struggle up a steep rise only to draw up at its summit, where Cree Bonner sat slumped in his saddle while staring angrily at black smoke curling up in the distance. Now the lake was spread out before them, and Bonner swung the gelding around so that it came down on its haunches, then fixed his eyes on Jed Starlight.

"There ain't no hope for her now, I reckon," he spat out. "Listen to me hard, son! You take that packhorse and skedaddle around to the other side of the lake. I'll make tracks for the cabin."

"I . . . I won't leave you alone!" he cried out.

Bonner jerked his head toward the western shoreline where several horsemen had appeared, and as the rest of the marauding Blackfeet came into view, he reached over and pulled the Winchester out of Starlight's hand, thrust the Hawken toward him. "Teal Eyes ain't with them murderin' bastards . . . which means that they

41

done her in."

"But ... but that doesn't mean they killed her."

"Dammit, boy, my heart tells me she's gone under. I've lost her ... but there's no sense in you going under too. Besides, your destiny lays out there on the plains — among your own people."

"We ... we could head south, Cree ... get away from them —"

"This ain't no time for jawing, boy!" Bonner said, as he struggled to keep his anger under control. "Don't you understand, Jed, I'm old — my bones tell me my time is up? You ... you've got your own destiny waiting. Now, dammit, boy, ride!" He struck Starlight's pinto with the stock of the Winchester, then watched intently as the man child he'd come to call his son fought to bring the running horse under control, saw Jed Starlight throw him a final pleading look.

"Now for them murdering bastards," Bonner declared. He cleared the trees and brought the gelding down onto the narrow strip of shoreline.

After Jed Starlight had gotten the pinto under control, he rode onto a rocky promontory overlooking the lake. From his high vantage point he could see Cree Bonner riding at a canter toward the approaching Blackfeet, the reins gripped in his teeth, both hands cradling the Winchester. Suddenly a cry of pain tore a hunk out of Starlight's heart when he saw one of the Indians hold up a silky mass of flowing black hair and let out a war cry, only to stiffen in shock as a slug from the mountain man's rifle thudded into his chest. Four more Indians toppled out of their saddles before gunfire from the others ripped the life from Cree Bonner.

Dusk was settling around Jed Starlight when he left

the place where he'd been holed up and found Cree Bonner's mutilated body. Bonner had been scalped, and his flesh gleamed red in the reflecting rays of sunlight. The Blackfeet had torn off most of his clothing, but the Shoshone amulet still hung around his neck. A sorrowful Jed Starlight removed it before trudging up toward the trees to dig a grave under a graceful aspen. After burying the mountain man, he returned to the cabin. All he found were smoldering ruins. The pole corral was empty. After looking around to see if he could find Teal Eyes' body, that she must have perished in the flames. It wasn't his way to cry or show his feelings too much, but what had happened today brought to the surface of his memory that other encounter with Indians.

"Why must there be such savagery?" he mused silently, bitterly. He recalled, also, that Teal Eyes had wanted him to go to her people if something happened to her, so, mounting his pinto, Starlight started on that long pilgrimage.

Nearly a month passed before Jed Starlight came upon a bluff overlooking a Shoshone village strung along the Green River. From Teal Eyes he'd learned the language of these people, and they'd spent a couple of winters with the Shoshones. Upon entering the village he soon found the lodge of Running Elk, Teal Eyes' elderly father. After Starlight had given his narration of what had happened, Running Elk came to the conclusion that the young white man must be permitted to stay until the bitterness left his mind, and he brought Jed Starlight to a lodge set off by itself.

"This is where you will live until your mind heals . . .

and your heart."

That said, Running Elk left Starlight, and later that night the young woman he had spoken to made her way to the lodge.

Arousing a slumbering Jed Starlight, she said simply, "I am Moon Calf." Then she disrobed, eased under the bearskin robe, and her warm, passionate body caused the troubled white man to forget his sorrow.

3

"You told me he was dead!"

The voice of Etta Montclair Lane lashed out at Terrapin who was standing passively by the closed door of her suite in the Frontier Hotel. A great dread had overcome her when he'd told her a blond-haired youth who'd fought Irish Jack O'Hara had a birthmark just like her husband's. Somehow she'd erased from her mind any recollection of Keno Lane's only son, Jed. But the young man she'd seen in front of the hotel had revived thoughts of Jed, and had brought Etta Lane to the harsh realization that everything she'd worked for all these years could be denied her if indeed this was Keno's blood kin come back from the dead.

"If that other hand hadn't of showed up, the kid would be dead," Terrapin said calmly, smoke from his Mex cigarette swirling around his glass eye.

"That's twice you've failed to carry out my orders!"

she cried out. Only Terrapin knew her true identity, carried with him the secret of how she'd managed to keep the ranch going. And the only reason Terrapin had stayed on at the ranch all these years was because — she sensed it — he was in love with her, though he'd never spoken of it. How could he even think, she silently asked herself, that I would let a brute like him make love to me? The gunhand knew too much, and Etta Lane feared his knowledge. Now that her husband had a good chance of being Wyoming's first governor, it was mandatory that she sever her ties with the past, and that meant getting rid of Terrapin.

She went to a window and gazed studiously at the main street aglow with lights. Her eyes moved to one of the banners strung across it, and a feeling of pride at what was printed on it surged through her. Etta Lane had become accustomed to power, money; and sometimes she found it hard to believe that nineteen years ago she'd been a young widow with two children to raise. Her outlaw husband had been killed during a bank holdup down in Colorado, but the other members of the gang, led by her brother, had gotten away. When her brother had given her some of the money taken in the robbery, she'd packed her few possessions and had taken a stage to Cheyenne.

It was in Cheyenne that she'd met Keno Lane, the legendary army scout turned rancher. During the early months of their courtship she'd helped him forget the sudden death of his young wife, and after they were married, Keno Lane had brought his new bride to the Rocking K, his ranch which was a vast spread in the Shoshone Basin. Mountain ranges like the Owl Creek, Bridger, Rattlesnake had became familiar landmarks

46

to her, and she had begun to want more for her family, to resent the hard fact that Keno favored his only son, had willed the ranch to him. He tolerated Etta's children, but rarely spoke to them. Nevertheless, Etta Lane was determined that her son Darby would inherit the ranch. And so she'd summoned her brother, the wily outlaw Cole Malone, who had willingly agreed to abduct Keno Lane's son. After the Malone gang, disguised as Indians, had raided the ranch, the task of killing Jed Lane had been assigned to Terrapin. Now anger simmered in Etta's eyes, for despite the gunhand's firm conviction that he'd killed the boy, she knew Jed was still alive.

After he'd lost his son, Keno Lane had sort of given up. He'd left the running of the ranch to the foreman, and to his wife. Chiefly, he could be found in saloons in either Grass Creek or Worland. He became even more distant from Etta's children, Darby and his younger sister, Crystal. And hard times came to the Rocking K, due to the terrible winter of '87 that saw many a ranch go under as cattle perished by the thousands, and to the unpaid bills Keno Lane accumulated because of his drunken sprees.

Turning away from the window Etta Lane went to the liquor cabinet and poured herself a glass of sherry while thinking about the deal she'd made with her outlaw brother. In the bloody months that had followed, the Malone gang had raided smaller ranches throughout the territory, killing those who resisted and driving the cattle to a valley hidden in the Big Horns. After the Rocking K brand had been burned onto the cattle, the herds had been turned over to Terrapin and other Rocking K hands, who'd driven

47

them to the railhead at Buffalo. From there they'd been shipped to Chicago. The Rocking K had prospered, and Etta Lane had bought out other ranchers in the basin. But there were those who refused to sell, and who accused the Rocking K of having a hand in the rustling, though they couldn't prove it. Keno Lane, unaware of his wife's role in the rustling, had hired some range detectives to hunt down the rustlers. Unwisely, though, he had confided in his wife, so the efforts of these men had resulted in only one arrest, that of a drifter named Downing who had no connection with Cole Malone's gang. He'd been hanged at Grass Creek, but his death had not stemmed the tide of rustling.

This had been done by Etta Lane when she'd learned that certain political leaders were seeking a man to run against the Republican candidate for governor. She'd sent word to her brother to lay low for a while, and then, through her efforts and somewhat against his natural desires, Keno Lane had been selected to be the Democratic candidate for governor at the convention in Sheridan. Through her husband, Etta Lane knew, her own star was rising.

Now her immediate problems were Terrapin and the young man with the birthmark. She forced a smile as she turned to the gunhand. "You realize, Terrapin, that if Keno finds out about this, he'll come gunning for you."

"Thought about that," he said curtly, and stepping over to the liquor cabinet, he pulled the cork from a bottle of brandy. "Thought about a lot of other things too."

His meaning was clear to Etta Lane: Terrapin

wouldn't hesitate to involve her in what had happened to Keno's son, or in the rustling. But she knew that out at the Rocking K Terrapin had led a pretty secure life, one that he wasn't about to forsake. When a man reaches his fifties, as Terrapin had, he is looking for a nest egg to fall back on. And he had strong feelings for her. But Etta Lane's desire for men, and that included Keno, had dried up. What lusty pleasures she got out of life came from the control she had over that Rocking K, and from her future plans for her son Darby. But she must never forget that Terrapin was a very dangerous man, one with absolutely no scruples, one who'd killed before. He'd been her contact with the Malone gang, and to Terrapin's way of thinking, that made them equal partners.

"You said that the wounded man was taken to the doctor's house. I figure the young man with the birthmark will be there too."

"Yup. Along with some of them Slash L hands. That kid just got lucky again."

"Dammit, Terrapin, it could be that he isn't Keno's son after all."

"I reckon you can't take that chance, Etta. Something else, too." He took a long swig from the bottle, a sudden smile crinkling the stubbled skin around his mouth, though there was no mirth in Terrapin's right eye and the other, the glass one, was staring off into a world all its own. "What wages you pay me ain't enough anymore."

Etta Lane had been expecting something like this. She refilled her glass while gazing at the hired gun. It would be too risky to ask one of the other hired guns to kill Terrapin. Somehow she'd have to do it herself.

49

But not now. More gunplay here in Rawlins could hurt her husband's political ambitions. Although the Democratic leadership had lent their support to Keno's campaign, their party was the smaller and less influential one in Wyoming. It lacked the financial support the cattle barons gave the Republicans. She'd contributed what she could from Rocking K funds, but a lot more money would have to be spent if Keno was to have any chance at all. That meant Terrapin would have to contact the Malone gang.

"Where's Cole holed up?"

"Hole-in-the-Wall, last I heard."

"Go to him. Tell Cole to start the rustling operation again."

"Could do that, Etta, but first there's this notion of mine that I'm to get a share in what's rustled."

"Go on?"

"Five bucks a head should set me up nicely."

"Why . . . that's way out of line!"

"Just remember, Etta," he said in a flat monotone, "I helped you get most of what you've got today, and when you're at the top of the heap, falling off can be mighty painful. Five bucks is a fair price, I reckon."

Irritably she tossed a lock of wavy black hair away from her eyes, then took a thoughtful sip from her glass. There was a rustle of silk as she turned away from him and moved around the overstuffed davenport to conceal her sudden flash of anger. How dare he be so impertinent, so damned cocksure. For the moment she would play his dangerous little game, but it wouldn't do to give in too easily. She said snappishly, "I don't like to be blackmailed, Terrapin."

"Consider it a form of life insurance," he responded.

Then he chuckled mirthlessly at what he'd said.

"Five, then!" She swung to face him. "But you'll have to kill this ... Jed Starlight."

"The kid's death warrant was signed a long time ago."

They laughed together, Etta exclaiming, "Too bad we can't blame the rustling on the Republicans."

"That could be arranged, too. I'll ride out at daybreak."

"We'll be leaving here before you get back, on the train to Rock Springs. Then we're heading to the Rocking K for a much-needed rest. Tell your men to keep an eye on Starlight, but they're not to kill him until we've left Rawlins."

After Terrapin's departure, Etta Lane paced the hardwood floor, her worry evident. That brief glimpse of Jed Starlight had brought back a greater fear than she had at first realized, as if she had seen a young Keno Lane. Perhaps it would have been better if Terrapin hadn't attended that prize fight at the side show, hadn't brought her the startling news of what he'd seen. Now something else wedged its unwelcome way into her worried thoughts as she became aware of another's presence. Yes, of course she'd closed the bedroom doors; now one of them stood ajar. It wasn't Keno's way to eavesdrop—so it must have been one of the children.

"Damn," she whispered, and quietly stole over and threw the door open, only to discover that the bedroom was unoccupied. Slipping around the bed, she opened the door to the corridor to find that empty too. The thought that it could have been Darby calmed her down some. She could confide in her son, trusted him far more than the pensive Crystal. Her daughter seemed to be slipping away, or could it be that running the ranch consumed so much of Etta's time and energy that she had little to give her daughter? Even though Crystal was a beautiful young woman and would make some rancher a fine wife, for Etta Lane the future was her son, Darby.

Often there were times when she reflected on her own painful early years, on how she and Cole had drifted from town to town eeking out a meager living. Then one dismal autumn day she'd helped Cole hold up a dry goods store in some nameless Kansas town. That had been the beginning of their robbing days. Others down on their luck had joined the Malone gang, and by the end of that year they'd hit several towns on a stretch from western Kansas into Colorado, leaving behind a few dead men and wanteds out on Cole and Etta Malone. She hadn't been looking for romance, but she hadn't been able to resist a tall Southerner with sensual eyes and a soft enticing drawl. There had been no marriage ceremony, just the two of them becoming a common-law couple, out of which two children were born. Things had been simpler then, knowing that sooner or later your fate was a bullet or the hangman's noose. There was a certain fever that got into your system from living that desperate life. Etta Lane knew she still hadn't quite shaken it. But it was different now, for she had the wealth, the power, to live as she wished. It was doubtful that anyone could tie her to those early reckless years. Her worry now was of a two-fold nature: Keno might find out his son was alive, and her involvement in the rustling might be exposed.

"Terrapin," she said doubtfully, "how much control do

you have over the other hired guns?" Though she'd gotten rid of those cowhands who'd been working out at the Rocking K when she'd first arrived, replacing them with a harder breed, she trusted none of the hands. Etta replied only in her iron will, her firm resolve that one day when people spoke of Wyoming they would mention the name Lane respectfully.

A cowhand loafing in front of the Rawlins town hall warned the crowd milling about on main street when a covey of men emerged from the building to, seemingly, from an honor guard for Keno Lane. He stood a head taller than the others, the light spilling out of the doorway revealing his quick smile as he waved casually. He had the gift of drawing others to him. His face, with the sandy-colored mustache masking the mouth, seemed composed, but those who'd waited for a glimpse of the famous Keno Lane could see steel flash out of those brown eyes. The gray Stetson was set at an angle, the sandy hair thick and trimmed so that it edged just above the collar of the tailored leather jacket. His smile singled out an old friend, and Keno called out, "Howdy, Jake, long time since we've bent elbows."

"Damned right, Keno, a long time. But you've sure enough got my vote."

Keno Lane slipped an arm around the shoulders of his campaign manager, Milt Prescott, a lawyer out of Sheridan, whispered, "Give my condolences to the mayor."

"But, Keno, you promised to go to that dinner and say a few words."

53

"We've covered most of the state. I'm talked dry, partner. I'm sure these people will understand." He strode away.

The truth of the matter was that Keno Lane wanted to get away from politicians and glad-handers, and for certain he didn't want to go back to the Frontier Hotel, for Etta would be there, that is, if she hadn't gotten tired of waiting and gone to the dinner scheduled to be held at the mayor's house. Keno was tired, burned out from the long miles he'd campaigned. Why had he let Etta talk him into this? In all of his fifty-two years he'd never seen a more ambitious woman, nor one who had so many infernal changes of mind. It was as if there were two people inside of Etta Lane, and he couldn't figure out either one. Out at the ranch they went to bed in separate bedrooms; another of Etta's confounded notions. She was still a handsome woman, but maybe all of that carousing he'd done since Jed had been killed had been too much for his wife. Could be that was it, although Jed's being gone all of these years had taken the spark out of Keno Lane too, and he knew it.

Once down in Cheyenne a woman had told him he had an animal magnetism. If that's true, he thought, I'm like a gelded horse—all show and no bottom. All he wanted to do at that moment was grab a fistful of the life he'd gotten used to, a good poker game and whiskey burning at his innards. There was also the woman who'd latched onto his growing army of supporters—Amanda Delaplaine, she called herself. She'd given a considerable sum to his campaign, and she'd confided to him this morning that she had a suite at the Daley House.

When Keno Lane reached the Plainsman Saloon, he paused to give his hat a lingering tug. Maybe a woman was what he needed instead of his usual form of entertainment, but the sounds coming from the saloon drew him inside and over to a poker table.

"Room for one more, boys?"

"Why, Keno, you old hoss thief. Make yourself comfortable."

"Much obliged."

4

The week had almost run its course, and on this Friday afternoon the sky was purpling over Rawlins. A southwest wind was sending dust devils skittering down the gravel road in front of the large brick house when Jed Starlight and the other Slash L hands gathered on the front porch were told that Mel Longstreet would pull through.

"It'll take him some time to recuperate," Dr. Goodwin went on.

They'd given what money they had left to the doctor, although Gar Lamont and those who hung out with him hadn't put in an appearance. The town marshal had logged down what had happened at Soo Ling's laundry as an attempted holdup, and though Starlight had been questioned, he'd kept his own notions to himself. He couldn't shake the feeling that he was being watched—especially that afternoon he'd gone downtown to find out that Keno Lane's entourage would be leaving for Rock Springs in the morning. It didn't seem natural that someone as important as

Lane needed hired guns. Perhaps these same men had killed the Chinaman?

Up in the mountains you sort of knew when it was going to storm, though there'd be no clouds showing at the moment; and again, something would warn you to hole up just before a roving band of Blackfeet came through. It wasn't much different down here, with hired guns taking the place of grizzlies and men sulking around like coyotes—they all left their own spore. According to frontier law, as detailed to him by the marshal, he'd need hard evidence before a warrant could be issued. In Starlight's estimation hard evidence would be the pelt of one of those killers draped over the marshal's desk. He'd never killed a man before, but somehow doing away with one of those coyotes wasn't all that unsettling when he considered what had happened to the Chinaman and Longstreet.

The other hands knew that Starlight had quit, and now one of them said, "Coming onto dusk, Jed, so I reckon we'll head out to the spread. But some of us will come in and keep Longstreet company."

"Jed, been a pleasure riding with you," another declared.

"Where you figure on heading in case you left some girl here in a bad way?"

Starlight laughed with the others, but their laughter was sort of quiet and they placed their boots carefully on the porch steps so that their spurs didn't jingle. He felt a lot lonelier when they climbed aboard their horses and rode away. The doctor's wife had asked them to stay for supper, and though good meals were hard to come by out there, it was a long ride out to the ranch. He'd miss them, no question about that.

In the settling dust left by their horses he looked past the lilac hedge in front of the house at the two dwellings across the gravel road. An elderly couple, the man crippled and hobbling about with the aid of a cane, lived in one of them, the other a clapboard house was boarded up. Alongside that was a vacant lot where weeds grew hip-high and then a larger building that had been abandoned, too. Beyond that were the backsides of the buildings strung along main street. Starlight had the uneasy feeling that a pair of eyes was stabbing at him through the ivy hanging from trellises to form a green rustling curtain over the open sides of the front porch. Probably belong to one of those who shot Longstreet, he thought.

He went inside and passed between an upright piano and a dining-room table covered with a lace tablecloth, on which silverware was set out for the evening meal. Crossing to the china cabinet with glass doors, he stood by the open bedroom door. Doctor Goodwin had just removed a thermometer from Longstreet's mouth, and he now held it up to read what it said in the wavering light cast by the lamp on the stand by the bed. The doctor was a sparse man with sunken cheeks partly hidden under a neatly-trimmed beard. The starched collar of his long-sleeved shirt pressed against his neck, and he wore round steel-framed glasses, their concave lens making his brown eyes appear larger than their actual size. He acknowledged Starlight's presence with an owlish glance.

"Improving some. But as I told you, it'll be a long spell before your friend sits a saddle. Terrible thing to happen." He thrust the thermometer into a shirt pocket, added mostly for his own benefit, "Should have stayed back East."

Longstreet coughed weakly before his eyes summoned Starlight into the room. "Just a flesh wound," he mumbled.

"They were after me," Starlight said, easing down on the chair.

"So you say." He dismissed the idea with a hand motion. "Jed ... don't blame yourself none ... for what happened."

"Got this feeling that you were right about trouble cropping up if I keep digging into the past."

"Too bad about Soo Ling."

"They've got to answer for that, too."

"Kid, don't you get no notions ... about hitting the avenging trail. Could be ... you'd get yourself killed."

"I suggest you get some sleep, Mr. Longstreet," said Goodwin, and he followed Starlight into the living room. He gestured tiredly for his guest to sit down at the table, settled himself at the end facing the front door, then pushed his glasses back into place on top of his long nose. "I detest this ... this violence."

"Sometimes these things can't be helped."

"This is a savage land," the doctor declared bitterly. "Should have stayed back in Pennsylvania. It isn't natural or civilized to have men going around carrying guns."

"Longstreet wasn't looking for trouble," Starlight said, as he tried to keep the resentment out of his voice. He smiled at the doctor's wife when she entered the room and set a platter of meat on the table before she settled down at his right.

How could he tell these people that he, too, was a stranger to the plains where the law of the gun held sway, not the genteel rules quoted to him by Colonel Avalon over at that side show. A bullet fired from a Winchester was a hell of a lot faster and could do far more damage than a right hook. This was the way of things out here, and in the mountains; and he'd have iron hanging from his hip until the time came when

59

the grizzly laid down with the Blackfoot. As the meal progressed, he got more of the same sermon from Mrs. Goodwin, a pinch-faced woman with snarly hair tied back in a bun. Her cynical words came in measured doses through a mouth about the size of a quarter. Though he knew that they were just taking their vexations out on him, he realized now why it was that Cree Bonner had disdained civilization – people just talked too damned much. And the doctor's wife was being stingy with the helpings of roast beef, though she kept piling undersized potatoes on his plate, and milk gone sour. He left the table with his stomach still growling some, and welcomed the solitude of the front porch, where he unbuckled his gun belt before taking off his boots. He stretched out on the hammock he'd been sleeping in ever since Longstreet had been brought to the Goodwins', and cupping his hands under his head, he let his thoughts drift to the town of Green River and a song he'd heard there. How did it go now? ... Yes, that was it – "Zip Coon." Closing his eyes, he hummed a few stanzas until a nearby clattering made him brace himself to rise from the hammock. Then a woman yelled something and a dog went yelping away. Settling himself again, Starlight drifted off to sleep.

Some three hours later the mental clock he'd set before falling asleep caused his eyes to pop open, and he stretched to rid himself of sleep before easing out of the hammock. First he snugged his feet into the pair of moccasins he'd taken out of his possible bag. Then he strapped on his gunbelt and settled his hat over his head. He passed a leather thong through the leather loops at the top of his boots before slinging them over his right shoulder and slipping off the porch to the dirt walkway. The town was quiet, shuttered down for the

60

night. There was no moon, and cloud cover hung low over Rawlins, but once in a while lightning flashed low to the southwest, while the smell of rain was in the air.

Crossing the road in a silent gliding walk, he pressed into the weeds growing in the vacant lot. Starlight's intention was to find out who'd been watching the doctor's house from that large deserted building he was approaching. He eased along its west wall until he came to a door hanging from its top hinge, then passed inside while reaching around for the Green River knife. Jed Starlight, the kid from the mountains, was doing what he did best, stalking a coyote with the deadly knife seemingly welded to his right hand, the left dangling free and near his holstered gun. Debris littered the sagging floorboards, but of their own volition, it seemed, his feet picked their way toward the front of the building without making any sound. Dimly he could make out someone seated on a packing crate near a front window, a rifle stacked against it, and whoever was seated there was sucking away at a quart bottle of whiskey. There was a sudden flare of lightning, and Starlight froze when the man ahead of him cursed and cast an anxious glance upward at a gaping hole in the roof.

"Damned stupid idea," the man said, and let out some curse words. "Especially since that kid ain't goin' riding tonight." When the bottle found his lips again, Starlight crept on.

Close like this, maybe three feet away, the rancid stench of the man came to him, and some tobacco smell. Then Starlight's left hand grabbed a hunk of greasy hair while his right brought the cutting edge of the blade around to settle against the man's throat.

"Uh . . . wha—"

"Easy, or I'll open you from ear to ear!"

61

"Wha . . . what do you want?"

"Who sent you here?"

"Nobody!" the man blurted out. "I . . . I needed a place . . . to bed down."

"I'll ask you one more time," Starlight said coldly, his knife drawing blood. "Who sent you here?"

"I . . . I just work for them is all."

"Them? Who is them?"

"Please . . . he'll kill me if I tell you!"

"The blade cut deeper. "You're a dead man if you don't!"

"Okay . . . okay . . . I work for . . . Terrapin."

Immediately Starlight thought of one of the men he'd seen escort that carriage into town, and he said, "Does this Terrapin have a glass eye?"

"That's him . . . that's Terrapin."

"And I'm the kid he told you to keep an eye on. Why?"

"Honest, kid . . . I just work for Terrapin. Please, that's all I know."

"What outfit do you ride for?"

"The Rocking K. Please, I'm just one of the hands."

"One of those who killed the Chinaman—bush-whacked a friend of mine."

"No, honest Injun . . . I had no part of that."

Though he knew the man was lying, Jed Starlight resisted the urge to slit his throat. Sooner or later the hired gun would get shot down by one of his own kind or a lawman, and besides, he needed the man alive—he wanted him to go back to Terrapin. Starlight said grimly, "I don't know why this Terrapin is gunning for me, scum. Just tell him that I'll be a lot harder to kill than a laundryman." Reaching for his revolver, he slammed its butt down hard on the man's head, and stepped away as he toppled into the dust.

Starlight made his way behind the buildings on main street, and when he reached the livery stable, he slipped inside through the back door. It was around four, with another two hours until sunup—two hours that would see him well on the way to Rock Springs. He was certain that Terrapin would take the train there, but if he chose to ride after Starlight, well, that would be all right too. As he reached for the saddle blanket, a slight rasping sound came to him where he stood by his bronc in the stall, and worriedly he scanned the other stalls, the wall ladder leading to the dark maw in the floor above where hay was pitched down.

"Starlight . . . is that you?"

It was a woman's voice, its melodious tones touched with a trace of uncertainty, and coming from up front. He didn't know what kind of game she was playing, and for certain there were she grizzlies down here too, so he pulled out his revolver and went to stand behind a ceiling beam that stall boards were nailed to.

"Who are you?"

"I . . . I followed you here this afternoon . . . when you came to look at your horse. Please . . . you must believe me . . . they mean to kill you."

"You mean Terrapin?"

"Yes, he's one of them!"

Somehow Starlight knew it was the young woman with the dancing hazel eyes flecked with gold specks, and a longing to see her overcame his caution. He stepped over the gutter and onto the dirt aisle running down the center of the stable, went to where she was standing, but with one hand gripping the door handle as if she wanted to flee.

He said, "How do I know you didn't bring someone with you?"

"Please, I'm alone. How did you find out about Terrapin?"

"From one of those coyotes he had keeping an eye on the doctor's house."

She opened the door a little more so that both of them were outlined in the light spilling in from the street and said questioningly, "Who are you?"

The way she asked that question took Starlight back some, because of the sudden fear in her voice. And how did she know his name? It seemed his coming here to Rawlins had spooked all kinds of people. In the dim light her eyes seemed to sparkle, her even rows of teeth were shining, and there was something familiar about the way she tilted her head as she talked. That picture of Sarah Bernhardt he'd seen in some saloon paled as he stared into her questing eyes, the memory of a younger, dark-haired girl such as this one clutching elusively at his mind. "Who am I?"

"Yes, you remind me of . . . someone I knew a long time ago."

"Guess that's a mystery I'm trying to solve. You knew my name. I'd like to know yours?"

"Crystal Lane. Jed, is it?"

"Yup, Jed Starlight."

An intensity such as he'd never seen before came into her eyes, and she said urgently, "Do you . . . do you have a birthmark on your . . . chest?"

"Got one." He touched his rib cage just below his heart. "The wing of an eagle, Cree Bonner called it."

She gasped, and then cried out, "Oh, my God! You're alive?"

"Course . . . I'm alive."

Closing the distance, she threw her arms around his neck, and he could feel her tears staining his shirt

64

front. "Oh . . . Jed . . . all of these years we thought—"

"You thought what?"

"You must get away!" she told him. "Now! There isn't time to explain. By now they're probably looking for me." She backed away, gathered up her skirts as she turned toward the open door. "You're in terrible danger, Jed. Please . . . leave while you can."

Then she was gone.

5

When cattle baron Tyler Barnett emerged from his Carey Avenue mansion, he turned satisfied eyes upon the other mansions strung along the street. These were the homes of men like him, some of whom rarely ventured out to their ranches. But Tyler Barnett made it a point to oversee every aspect of his ranching operation down near Laramie. He was of average size, a pearl gray cattleman's hat settled over his mane of iron-gray hair. A meticulous dresser, he had on a burgundy velour coat over a black vest with mother-of-pearl buttons, and creased black trousers tucked into calfskin boots. The rancher was a Republican. That was his reason for going to the Cheyenne Club on this dismal rainy night. The driver swung the buggy away from the carriage house and over to the back porch, and Barnett crouched into its covered interior.

As the buggy rolled through the quiet streets of Cheyenne, Tyler Barnett wondered if the man he had summoned would show up. The other members of the committee had better be there or, come tomorrow, there'd be hell to pay. Barnett was concerned about the growing support being given Keno Lane's campaign. He'd listened to the bar talk, the gossip going around Cheyenne and other towns; knew that Gatchell, the Republican candidate for governor, would lose the election unless drastic measures were taken. But he had to give the Democrats credit for picking a living legend as their gubernatorial candidate.

"Keno Lane's a spellbinder," he said grudgingly. Barnett didn't consider himself a vindictive man, though his enemies would say otherwise; but he realized that Keno Lane's political machine must be stopped despite the cost to the Republican Party, even if that meant killing the rancher.

At the corner of Seventeenth and Warren, the driver pulled up before a large pretentious building, the Cheyenne Club, which since its construction in 1880 had become a Wyoming landmark. The clubhouse had a mansard roof with five chimneys poking skyward, two full-length verandas, and, out front, a couple dozen hitching posts. It was surrounded by elm trees. This was where the cattle barons came to socialize, make deals, do their politicking.

"I'll have someone else take me home," Barnett said, as he eased himself out of the carriage and hurried up the wide porch steps and into the clubhouse.

"Good evening, sir," the servant said, reaching to take Barnett's hat.

Barnett nodded, handed it over, and proceeded along the hallway. Coming to the barroom, he glanced inside to see if any members of his committee were there. He knew the two ranchers sitting at a table. At another, by himself, was Ramsey, a reporter for the *Cheyenne Leader*, while standing at the bar were a couple of

67

legislators, men whom Barnett took special pains to do favors for. Daley, one of the legislators, had voted for the Maverick Law, one of the major weapons the cattle barons had in their efforts to keep out nesters and small ranchers. That law stated that stray cattle, or mavericks, those without brands, must be rounded up in the spring, and then only by the cattle barons, who'd divide the cattle among themselves. But smaller ranchers and those wanting to get into the cattle game were brazenly ignoring the law by simply going out at any time and claiming what cattle they found. Like the silversmiths of Diana, their craft was in danger, and so the cattle barons created a black list of suspected stock thieves, their term for those who didn't belong to the Wyoming Stock Growers Association.

It was under the auspices of this association that Barnett had called this meeting, because of a new danger that had sprung up—rustling. Chiefly, the rustlers had confined their activity to the Wind River and Big Horn basins. Barnett had sent some stock detectives up to Worland and Sweet Grass, and their findings had led him to believe that the Rocking K could be involved in the rustling. He'd also been informed that Keno Lane spent a lot of time in these towns.

As Barnett moved on toward the reading room where the meeting was to be held, he fished from an inner coat pocket a folded newspaper clipping he'd taken from the *Denver Star*. Unfolding the yellowing piece of paper, he stared at the picture on it—a man astride a big bay with a white star on its forehead.

"Ezra Philby," he murmured. Somehow the name didn't conjure up images of a gunfighter, and neither did the appearance of the man astride the horse. The horseman had a round face and tufted brows, and he had on a black suit like a minister's or like someone would wear to attend the funeral of a relative. His hat was black too, and somewhat shapeless. And if Philby did wear a gun it was tucked under the folds of the black coat. Philby's eyes were what held Tyler Barnett's gaze now, for they told a different story, that of a man who could deal out death without blinking them. Philby had earned the sobering nickname The Executioner, and justifiably so because of all the outlaws he'd jailed, or hanged. His official title was U.S. Marshal Ezra Jehoahaz Philby. A student of the Bible, Barnett recalled how another Jehoahaz after becoming ruler of ancient Judah received bribes from the moneylenders, the powerbrokers of those days. A reliable source had informed the rancher that Marshal Philby could be bribed also.

Upon entering the reading room, Barnett included the five men gathered there in a curt nod as he took out his gold turnip-shaped watch; in another minute it would be eight o'clock. He'd briefed these men about what to expect tonight, and their presence meant that if murder had to be done, it had their tacit approval.

A buffet table had been set up, and one of the ranchers was mixing drinks behind a portable bar — Bennington, from up Stony Creek way. The ranchers were lean men with the stamp of the outdoors ingrained on their faces, hard of eye, and with the easy movements all outdoorsmen seem to acquire. The shelves strung along one wall contained Eastern newspapers — *Harper's Weekly* and *Monthly*, the *New York World*, *Boston Sunday Herald*, and *New York Daily Graphic*. Most of them invested heavily in Eastern enterprises, but mainly they read the *Cheyenne Leader* or *Denver Star*.

"Say, Jess," said a rancher named Colbert, "I saw that opera last night . . . *The Bohemian Girl*. Expected more than a fat woman covered from head to toe and hollering at the top of her lungs."

"Maybe you'd better stick to more familiar surroundings, like whorehouses."

"They sure holler there, too."

Tyler Barnett laughed with the others as he poured some St. Cruz rum over the ice cubes he'd put in his glass. But he drank sparingly, for this was a special occasion. Then Barnett, like the others, felt the presence of someone else, and everyone turned to look at the door. It stood open now, the man standing in the frame studying those who'd summoned him from Colorado Springs.

"You, of course, are Barnett," the stranger said.

Tyler Barnett felt a tremor of unease under the impact of Marshal Ezra Philby's gaze. The man's eyes were harder than what the photograph had captured, black as coal. The penetrating glitter in them made Barnett and everyone in the room forget about Philby's rumpled black suit.

"You're Bennington," Philby went on, his glance holding the rancher's eyes. "You're Colbert . . . Jess Ramsey . . . Watson . . . you, Milbank out of Sheridan." He removed his hat to reveal dark brown hair parted in the middle and curling around his ears.

Barnett had never met the marshal before, and from the uneasy looks on the others' faces, neither had the members of the committee. He gestured nervously toward the long polished oaken table, mumbled, "We might as well get to the business at hand," though he was left with the feeling that Marshal Philby had taken control of the meeting. As he pulled out the

70

chair at one end of the table, Philby reached for the chair at the other end of it.

"Marshal, would you like a drink?"

"No," came Philby's flat reply.

"So, then," Tyler Barnett said after everyone had settled down, "you seem to know something about all of us?"

"Enough." Marshal Philby lifted a cigar out of a shirt pocket. "I have my vices, too." He lit it with a wooden match.

Barnett said, "I've been told that you're looking to build up your . . . retirement fund."

"Among other things."

"And you also probably know that we represent the Wyoming Stock Growers Association, that our reason for asking you to come here, sir, is to rid our state of rustlers."

"Oh"—cigar smoke billowed out of Marshal Philby's wide mouth to engulf Colbert seated to his right—"you're members of the association, I know. But it isn't the association that wants to avail themselves of my services and those of my men. Place your cards on the table, Mr. Barnett."

Tyler Barnett's lips pursed in anger, and he carefully placed his glass to one side, stared intently at Philby. "This state is infested with rustlers, which you're well aware of, sir. The center of this activity appears to be up in the Big Horn basin."

"Milbank spoke up. "That's right. Us folks up Sheridan way have been hit hard by rustlers."

"I have reason to suspect," Barnett said, "that the Rocking K is involved in this."

"Keno Lane's place," said Philby, and flicked cigar ashes on the floor.

"If he is involved, that would simplify our problem."

"Yup, it sure would make things easy for the Republicans."

"Yes, well, Marshal Philby, we're prepared to offer you a handsome sum of money to ... to take care of this problem," Barnett responded.

"Make it clear!" Philby retorted.

Now the eyes of the other ranchers swung to Barnett, and some of them edged forward on their chairs. Barnett cleared his throat before he said, "The members of this committee have agreed"—there, he mused cagily, I've made certain my fellow ranchers understand their position in this—"that Keno Lane must not win the election ... that he must be ... killed."

"That's clear enough," Philby said. "Now to the gist of what I want. From each of you ... five thousand dollars—plus another five thousand to cover my expenses."

"Why ... that's thirty-five thousand," retorted Milbank.

"It's too damned much!"

A hired gun'll do it for a hundred bucks and a steak supper."

"It's cheap enough," Philby lashed out, "when you gentlemen consider that you'll be gaining control of a state. A bargain, I call it. Well?"

"I tell you, it's too damned much!"

"Simmer down!" said Tyler Barnett. "Philby's right; it's cheap enough when you consider what would happen if Lane won the election."

Rising, Marshal Ezra Philby put on his hat and dropped on the table the card he'd just taken out of his coat pocket. "Before I do anything, gentlemen, the money will be deposited in the First National Bank of Denver under the name you'll find on that card."

"We must have the guarantee," said Barnett, "that no one outside of this room finds out about our involvement in this."

"I expect as much from you, gentlemen."

"Once the money is deposited, where can we reach you?"

"Here in Cheyenne, the Fairmont Hotel. No, stay where you are, Mr. Barnett, I'll find my way out."

After Marshal Philby had left the clubhouse, he cut across the intersection and went down Seventeenth Street to a carriage that had been waiting for him. Opening the door, he sat down beside a tall somber man clad in a brown suit and derby, and Philby said softly, "Struck a deal."

"When do we head out?"

"Soon's the money reaches the bank." He related to Deputy U.S. Marshal J. D. Murdock the pertinent details of what had transpired in the Cheyenne Club. "Sort of convenient for Tyler Barnett and those other Republicans back there that the Rocking K is located in the middle of rustling activity."

"Maybe too convenient?"

"My thoughts." Murdock clucked the horses out into the street. "I wonder how the federal judge feels about entrapment, which is about what we're trying to do to them ranchers."

"It's been my experience that those so-called honest folks who've got larcenous minds generally entrap themselves. Anyway, we might set a legal precedent for future generations."

"Could be at that. So what if the Rocking K has turned against the law?"

"Got my job to do."

"And if it hasn't, Keno Lane might live to rocking chair age."

"Cross that bridge when I come to it."

6

The land west of Rawlins unrolled over the Great Divide Basin, mostly a vast area of mesas and cacti and prairie, with a few ravines and creeks. From one of the higher elevations, Jed Starlight viewed a passenger train heading westward. Secured to a flat-bed car was the carriage he'd seen back in Rawlins, and he knew Keno Lane and his family were aboard the train.

He was in no particular hurry, for Keno Lane would do some politicking in Rock Springs; and he was leaving a trail for Terrapin and his men to follow. Starlight was in a daydreaming mood, his thoughts on the young woman who'd come upon him at the livery stable. She'd left him with a glimpse of a past he could scarcely remember, and a craving to get a good look at Keno Lane. It would sure shake the acorns off the old oak tree, Jed pondered, if Keno turned out to be his father. The brief time she'd clung to Jed had set his heart to thumping, but why did his presence in

Rawlins make damned near everyone want to do him harm? Strange that she should know about the birthmark. But daydreaming, Cree Bonner had told him enough times, could separate a man from his scalplock, so shaking that glazed look out of his eyes, Starlight pivoted easily and studied the lay of the land eastward. For nearly fifteen minutes the only things moving atop rimrock were Jedekiah Starlight's searching eyes and his horse, which was nuzzling for a few clumps of short grass. Finally his patience was rewarded by what appeared to be a line of ants inching across a stretch of open plain.

By his reckoning Starlight had at least a three-hour head start on those coming along his backtrail. The position of the sun told him it was going on midafternoon, and though the train would pull into Rock Springs sometime after nightfall, for a horseman it was a two-day journey. His purpose now was to leave no tracks for his pursuers to find, a task for which Jed Starlight was eminently qualified. Chucking his horse into motion, he rode off the sloping wall of the mesa and headed for a dry wash meandering westerly.

The fire made by one of Terrapin's men blazed tall to reflect against a sheltering rock wall below which a sluggish creek flowed. The water, to their dismay, was dirty, brackish, but their mounts seemed to relish what they had drunk. At a dry ford back about fifteen miles, they'd lost the tracks left by Jed Starlight's horse, even though one of them, a half-blood out of the Cherokee Nation, had been riding at point. And Terrapin's anger was visible for everyone to see.

"Dammit, he's only a kid!" he said. "And you damned fools call yourselves trackers!"

"He may be a kid," said Burt Logan, the half-blood,

"but he's more man than us when it comes to hiding his trail." He went back to whittling on a piece of wood.

"Maybe so," said Terrapin, "but, Woodley, if you hadn't been sucking on that whiskey bottle—"

"Shucks, Terrapin, I was keeping an eye on that doctor's house."

"—we'd be aboard that train and coming onto Rock Springs about now."

"Just what is so damned important about killing that kid?"

Casting his brooding eye the half-blood's way again, Terrapin spat out, "None of your business, Logan. Just do as you're told. Anybody thinks otherwise can just ride the hell out."

Terrapin sat by himself, away from the campfire and with his back propped up on his saddle, a bottle of whiskey at hand, but he drank sparingly, What had been hammering at his mind since early summer was his future. He'd grown bone weary of working for Etta Lane, putting up with the woman's high-handed ways, and spending nights with hard men like these whose only notions were a craving for money and for places to spend it. All of them had at one time or another gunned someone down, and for certain, Terrapin mused, if Etta gave the order they'd come after him. This always having to be on one's guard was getting to him, and he knew it. With a bankroll he could head back East, maybe, spend his graying years as the proprietor of a proper saloon. That idea chased away some of his anger.

"Might's well tell you now as later," he finally rasped. "It seems we're back in the rustling business." His announcement brought forth a few pleased grins.

"Politicking, I hear," Logan said sagely, "can get damned expensive."

"Especially if you're on the short end of the stick."

"Meaning you don't think Keno has a chance of winning the election?"

"Etta Lane ain't gonna let that happen. Come sunup, Logan, you and Hadley make tracks over to Hole-in-the-Wall and get together with Cole Malone."

"What if Cole ain't there?" questioned Hadley, a beefy man with stringy black hair hanging to his shoulders.

"Then find him!"

"Reckon we can do that," Logan said calmly. "But this means that you'll have to hire more men."

"You're getting to sound more like a ramrod every day, Logan," Terrapin muttered angrily. Keeping his sighted eye on Logan, he drank deeply from the bottle, wiped the spillage from his speckled beard. "I figure either at South Pass City or Atlantic City we'll find some hombres who couldn't cut the oil game."

"Yup," ventured Woodley, "that stuff can sure stink a man up."

"So we're back to rustling," said the half-blood. "I've been wondering if Cole Malone is really that good with a gun."

"Malone's fast all right," said Terrapin. "We need him, Logan, so don't do anything stupid. Now, enough yammering. Get some shut-eye 'cause we're heading out before first light."

The men slithered into bedrolls which until now had been kept tied into tight rolls, for only a greenhorn would leave his unrolled on the ground, giving a rattler an opportunity to crawl inside in search of a warm place to spend the night. No guard was posted since these hardcases felt no harm could come to men who made a living with the gun, not from a band of Indians or from some damnfool kid. The fire slackened off, and the horses, tied to a picket line, stopped switching about and settled in as the summer moon occasionally poked out from between drifting gray clouds. Farther along the creek a coyote trotted up to the stream and began to lap up water. And the night cooled with the quickness found only in high plateau country.

Another hour elapsed before there was a stir of movement on the rock wall offering shelter to the sleeping Terrapin and his men. Then a shape took form, a shadowy one blending in with other shadowy forms of the night. It lost its vagueness as the moon scudded away from a screening cloud to reveal Jed Starlight clad in his doeskin suit, moccasins on his feet, and hatless so that moonlight brightened his crown of blond hair. Carefully he found toe- and hand-holds on the cold rock wall, then he began to inch down its rough face. So silent was his descent that the horses didn't cock curious ears his way, and from what Jed had seen while eavesdropping from his rocky perch, the senses of the men below were dulled by liquor, and by a hard arrogance resulting from their own prowess with the gun.

Encountering loose rock and gravel at the base of the wall, he came onward cautiously to pad silently past one of the sleeping hardcases who was snoring drunkenly. Out of Starlight's sheath came his Green River knife when he came upon Terrapin sprawled on his side in his bedroll, a six-gun near the man's open hand, his weather-stained hat pulled low over his head which was resting on the worn cherry-leather saddle.

"How easy it would be," Starlight pondered in Shoshone, "to slit the man's throat, kill the others." But cold-blooded murder didn't come naturally to him, nor was he seeking scalplocks, even though these men were the men who'd gunned down Mel Longstreet. Warily he came around in a searching crouch, turned his attention back to Terrapin when he saw that his

79

presence hadn't disturbed the slumber of the others.

Easing around the sleeping man, Starlight slipped to his knees and began to carve the letters of his first name into the saddle. Then he hesitated, stilling the urge to do harm to the man he believed had left him to die those many years ago. The memory of that night came and went, as did the flaming embers in Jedekiah Starlight's eyes. This man, he knew, could bring him to those who had ordered his death. And then, shadow-like, he was in among the horses, whispering in Shoshone to calm them. Untying the picket line, he brought the mounts at a careful walk through the brush screening the creek, onto prairieland, and over to the small rocky point where he'd left his own horse. Springing into the saddle, and with the other horses still tied to the picket line he was holding, Starlight cantered southwesterly toward some foothills behind which the Uinta range loomed.

"Sleep well, Terrapin, for my dealings with you have just begun."

Our horses, they're gone!"

"What do you mean, gone?" Terrapin yelled back, as he struggled out of his bedroll and lurched to his feet.

"Sonofabitch!" moaned Hadley, who'd gone to see about the horses. "They've been rustled, Terrapin. We should'a had someone standing watch."

Out of their bedrolls came the others, all going to where the horses had been picketed. They fanned out searching for sign in the uncertain light of early dawn. Then the half-blood, Logan, threaded the shallow creekwater and on the opposite bank followed the trail left by Starlight in the brush. When he came back a few minutes later, he found the others clustered by the water, but he didn't speak until he'd recrossed the creek.

"One man did it," Logan said quietly to Terrapin. "Found some moccasin tracks."

"I knew there was some Cree sulking around these parts," snarled Woodley.

Controlling his anger, Terrapin finally muttered, "No sense crying over spilled bacon grease. How far are we from the railroad line?"

"I'd say, five miles at the most."

"I don't relish a long walk either, but damned if I'll do it on an empty stomach. Get that fire going, Woodley."

Burt Logan glanced across the creek, then back at Terrapin. "Think the kid did it, this Jed Starlight?"

"It was Injuns, Logan, pure and simple. And that's the story we tell when we get to Rock Springs."

After eating the Rocking K hardcases hefted their saddles and rifles, and trailed out at a reluctant walk which would eventually bring them to the Union Pacific's main line. As was their custom, the half-blood walked out front, and the ramrod Terrapin was last in a ragged line of bitter men. Less than an hour passed before they stopped to unbuckle their spurs and take a breather. Feet not accustomed to walking over such rugged terrain were starting to ache. But soon on they went. At one point Woodley's right boot found a gopher hole and he tumbled to the ground, his saddle landing heavily on his back.

Without breaking stride Terrapin went on past him, saying, "Make damned sure you don't leave your saddle, Woodley."

The hardcase threw Terrapin an angry look. Then he regained his feet, picked up his saddle, and started after the others. Suddenly a curious glint danced in his squinting eyes when he chanced to notice the fresh markings on Terrapin's saddle, and he brought this to

81

the man's attention.

"Markings?" snapped out Terrapin. "What the hell are you talking about?"

"Yeah, it looks like someone carved his initials in it."

Unslinging the heavy saddle from where it had been riding on his brawny shoulder, Terrapin dropped it at his feet and leaned over quizzically. "Jed," he read. "That kid . . . rustled our horses?"

"Ain't no Injun I know of can write?"

"Okay, Terrapin," said Burt Logan, "I figure it's time you told us what this is all about — why you want this kid gunned down and just who in tarnation he is."

The men fell silent while staring at Terrapin, but he was not a man to be easily stampeded. By nature he was tight-lipped, and he had no close friends. None of these men had been around during those early years, so they were unaware that Keno Lane had sired a son, nor did they know that Keno had been some kind of tracker before whiskey and a soft life had dulled his talent. Some Indians, either Shoshone or northern Cheyenne, must have found Keno's son staked out and left to die, taught him their ways. That Jed had turned up now was downright eerie, but he owed these hardcases no explanation as to why the kid had to die.

"You're paid to keep your lips buttoned, and to use your guns when you're called upon to do so." A brazen smile appeared on his face. "There's something else we've got to consider. Just when did that kid find our camp? I figure he overheard us talking about hooking up with Cole Malone to do some rustling. Which means that each of you has a personal stake in seeing him dead and buried."

"Reckon Terrapin's right. He could tell what he knows to some U.S. Marshal."

"You've earned an *A* for effort, Hadley. So it's either get that kid . . . or get strung up for rustling. Just to sweeten the pot, boys, there's an extra five hundred to the man who kills Jed Starlight. Now, let's vamoose before those buzzards circling overhead pay us a visit."

7

Rock Springs was just another hardscrabble railroad town that had taken hold when a lot of others had gone under, and close enough to the Utah line to hear the religious murmurings of the Mormon sect, that is, if one had spiritual leanings. It was a milkstop for those passing through on their way west, a supply point for neighboring ranchers and the like. Its few attractions, out on this treeless plateau, were saloons and dance halls, so any celebration, be it of a civic or political nature, was welcomed. Somehow the town fathers had found enough in their coffers to purchase some fancy bunting and the flags which adorned the buildings along the boardwalks on main street, while at the Union Pacific telegraph office, operators were kept busy sending messages brought to them by both candidates for governor, messages which would eventually find their way into the territorial newspapers. Mostly these communications contained lies told by one candidate about another, but some gave voters of wavering minds just a hint of the platforms the candidates advocated.

Into the excitement of this political campaign, along flag-lined main street, rode five horsemen, the afternoon sun beaming into eyes no longer shaded by the brims of their hats as they tipped their heads back to scan the rooftops and upper windows in that fashion peculiar to men on the dodge or those upholding the law. Needless to say, the six-pointed badges of U.S. Marshal Ezra Philby and his deputy marshals weren't showing. But the few gamblers and hardcases fortunate enough to catch a glimpse of Philby's entourage cutting onto a side street and heading toward the livery stable knew without voicing it that the law had come to Rock Springs. And those with paper out on them began making hurried arrangements to leave town.

Marshal Philby had already laid out a course of action for his deputies. First of all, J. D. Murdock, a rather tall man with drooping eyelids and an undistinguished appearance, would latch onto the coattails of the charismatic Keno Lane. Judging from Murdock's attire he could be a drummer; in fact, he'd been one before hooking on as a deputy marshal. The other three deputies would keep an eye on Keno Lane's supporters and family. This would leave Philby free to float through the saloons, choice places to pick up information. A devout Baptist, there was still a hankering in him for an occasional drink of hard liquor or a turn or two with the cards, and in his shirt pocket could always be found two or three choice cheroots.

In his shapeless black suit, the wilted collar of his white shirt folded over a string tie, Ezra Philby drew few glances as he wandered from saloon to dance hall. The presence of the political candidates, he couldn't help noticing, had brought in the usual element of floaters, drifters, and easy-money artists. But Philby was after bigger game, though if he came across a wanted criminal he'd have to do his lawful duty.

The supper hour brought no rush from the saloons to seek out food, since most of these places furnished a sort of buffet, and while standing at the bar in Casey's Riverboat saloon, Philby sampled a hunk of hard cheese and summer sausage. Just a block away was Keno Lane's campaign headquarters in the spacious Great Western Hotel. And just beyond the pair of cowhands standing to Philby's right a drunken railroad worker was trying to refill his shot glass from a bottle under the critical eye of the mustachioed bartender hovering behind the crowded bar. The saloon was only a big, boxy room filled with poker tables and other gambling impedimenta, a player piano yowling away in a murky corner. Turning to drape an elbow on the bar top, Philby eyed those gathered around a faro table, where a bandy-waisted peddler was trying to "buck the tiger" as he played alone against the gambler presiding over the faro layout. The peddler seemed to be winning, judging from the number of poker chips stacked before him. Keep it up, bucko, Philby commented mutely, and you'll leave here busted and shoeless.

Tiring of the continuous wailing of the player piano, and of the unsavory aromas in Casey's Riverboat saloon, Philby shoved his boots through sawdust and out onto the boardwalk. While puffing on his cigar, he surveyed the crowded street for any sign of his men or the others he was seeking. The food he'd partaken of in the saloon hadn't sated his hunger pangs, for it was the marshal's habit to have a plentiful evening meal around nine o'clock.

Perhaps it had been a waste of time, detouring over here to Rock Springs instead of heading directly for Keno Lane's Rocking K spread. With luck, and if, indeed, Keno was involved in rustling, Philby might have stumbled across some running irons, which would be all the evidence he needed to place the rancher behind bars.

Cattle baron Tyler Barnett wanted Lane dead and buried, and men such as Tyler Barnett generally made the rules in this kind of game, twisting them to suit their purposes. As Philby had insisted, the money paid him by Barnett and his cronies had been deposited in a Denver bank; there it would remain until he'd cleared Keno Lane or sent him to prison or worse.

Crossing over, Philby worked his way past an emporium displaying women's apparel in its wide front windows. Then he headed downstreet. He walked with a slight stoop to his shoulders, as men do when they're getting on in age or their minds are laden with wearying thoughts. But hardened as he was to the trail, Ezra Philby could outride much younger men, and come sunup of another day, he'd head out, relentless until he caught his quarry. As he started rehashing the background of rancher Keno Lane, the distant shrilling of a train whistle came to him, and staring at a clock in the window of a haberdashery Philby noticed it was coming onto nine o'clock. Venturing across an intersection, he turned down a quieter side street, to enter a small Mexican restaurant and settle down at a large table.

Within the half-hour all of his deputies had wandered in, and one of them, J. D. Murdock, was detailing briefly what he'd learned while observing the candidate Keno Lane at close range. "About all I've found out is that Lane can talk the buttons off a brass monkey. Seems sincere enough about what he intends on doing if elected. The other candidate, that Republican, sure can cover up his tracks with a wordslide; he's one of those who likes to talk out of both sides of his mouth."

"Did you see any of Barnett's crowd over there?"

"Not that I recollect, Ezra."

"But I seen some interesting gents get off the train." Everyone glanced at Rufus Owsley, a square-jawed Oklahoman short on words but keen of eye. "Judged them to be owlhooters. Carried saddles, they did. Seemed nettled to be doing so—like hard times had fallen upon them." He spooned more sugar into his coffee mug, and stirred it three or four times. "Anyways, one of them gents—I later established that he's a tough hombre named Terrapin—took it upon himself"—Owsley took a swig of coffee—"to call upon a woman staying at the Great Western."

"Just who would this damsel be, Rufus?"

"At the time it seemed strange, this Terrapin sneaking into the hotel through a back door." Shifting in his chair, Rufus Owsley drank from his mug. "But it began to make sense when I found out just who it was that had taken up residence in that suite over at the Great Western."

"Now, Rufus," chided Marshal Philby, "I don't want to have to go around the barn to get an answer to my question—"

"He went a-calling on Keno Lane's missus—was still there when I left and came here."

"This Terrapin . . . he got a glass eye?"

"Same gent, Marshal."

"Back a few years, as I recollect," murmured Philby, "Terrapin was mixed up in unlawful activities down in Kansas. Got sentenced to ten years, hard labor."

"Now he's head honcho out at the Rocking K spread."

"Sets me to wondering," said Ezra Philby as he rose and donned his hat. "Go ahead and enjoy your meal, gentlemen. I must be alone to collect my thoughts about this. Oh, Clarkson, did you secure lodging for us?"

"Over at the Big Horn Hotel, sir."

"Fine . . . fine."

"Marshal Philby."

"Deputy Marshal Owsley?"

"Missus Lane was alone in the suite when Terrapin went up there. Probably not important mentionin' that, though."

Grimacing, Ezra Philby strolled outside and, at the first corner he came to, paused to light a cigar. The only thing unusual about Terrapin's presence in Keno Lane's suite was his method of getting there, because those who worked for large ranchers had a habit of strutting in the front entrance. And there was the incident at Rawlins. The marshal of that railroad town had given Marshal Philby descriptions that pretty much matched the bunch working for Terrapin. While the doctor who'd treated that wounded hand, Mel Longstreet, had told Philby about a strange young man, a friend of Longstreet's named Jed Starlight. For a fact, Philby knew that shortly after Starlight had left Rawlins, Terrapin and his men had trailed out on horseback. Why they should show up here, and come in on the train, was a puzzle that Philby meant to solve. The one called Starlight might have stolen their horses. But he was no more'n a yonker. Somehow, though, this yonker—Jed Starlight—was the key to this whole thing.

Coming to a bench in front of a dry goods store shuttered for the night, Philby sat down, and folded one leg over another, and then stretched an arm on the back rest. Upstreet he had a clear view of the Great Western and the businesses beaming with lights. The streets were still crowded, but the numbers were thinning some, and judging from the sounds trickling out of the saloons and dance halls the spirit of this political campaign had gotten to most everyone. At times this could be a harsh land of wintry storms or summer drought; and Philby didn't begrudge these folks the fun they were having tonight. He set his thoughts back a couple of months, to a secret meeting he'd had in Denver with Judge John C. Darett. . . .

The air in the judge's chambers were stuffy due to the windows being nailed down—Darett suffered from asthma. Behind where Philby sat in a hard-backed chair facing a desk cluttered with legal documents, one door opened into the courtroom, another into an inside corridor trailing to the rear entrance, but curiosity held Philby's eyes on a third door. It stood ajar and opened into a bedroom and connecting bathroom. Marshal Philby, having scouted out the comings and goings of everyone during the day, knew that someone else had been invited to this meeting, but he'd hear the judge out before making an issue of it.

Although it was only midafternoon and he had a full docket of cases, Judge Darett had adjourned court for the day. He hadn't bothered to remove his black robe, and as a result sweat was beginning to film his smoothly shaven face. Darett's hair was parted exactly in the middle, combed back along the sides of his large head in thick rusty strands showing traces of gray. The small grooves on both sides of his flaring nose had been caused by wearing reading glasses. Though of average height and appearance, John C. Darett was said to possess one of the finest legal minds west of the Mississippi, a evaluation that Marshal Philby heartily disagreed with. But like all barristers, Darett was, in Philby's opinion, prone to favor the party of his political leanings.

"Rustling seems to have gotten out of hand up there,

Philby."

"Up there" meant Judge Darett was speaking of territorial Wyoming. A younger man or one not accustomed to the judge's heavy-handed sarcasm would have responded in kind or stalked out. Philby merely nodded while flicking a fly away from his hat. Ear-burning experiences told him the judge usually ran out of wind after five minutes or so, whereupon he'd reach for the decanter of rye hidden behind some books piled untidily on a wooden file cabinet. Another bad habit the judge had was picking away with his tongue at an empty tooth socket. Marshal Philby had already been on the job a good fourteen months when Darett had arrived to replace the venerable T. O. Aldridge, a seasoned Westerner, now pining away at the Veterans' Home back in St. Louis.

"Much as I hate to say it," Judge Darett went on, "some of the cattle barons could be involved."

"Some of them are," retorted Philby.

"The bigger ranchers control township and county elections; as a result the crooked sheriff is the rule rather than the exception. These ranchers accuse the nesters and sodbusters of rustling just to cover up their own crimes. The law, Philby, is held up to mockery. New measures are needed—which is where you come in. I've let it be known to a few unsavory characters that you can be bribed."

"That's mighty noble of you, your honor," the marshal said testily.

"There's a legal device called entrapment."

"Heard of it," Philby said. In a broad sense, he recalled, it meant an officer of the government induced a person to commit a crime he had not contemplated so that same person might be prosecuted for the offense. But just what did this have to do with rustling? He nodded toward the bedroom door. "Suppose

91

you quit shuffling that deck of legal mumbo jumbo and trot Governor Randall out here."

"You're a clever man," said Judge Darett. "Perhaps, too clever."

The door swung open and the territorial governor of Wyoming, an evasive smile on his face, stepped up to the desk. But there was a certain shrewdness in Warner Randall's probing eyes. "As you know, Marshal Philby, people up in Wyoming have a nasty habit of interpreting the law in ways that suit their own purposes. So we've decided to fight fire with fire. Some of the bigger ranchers, acquaintances of mine, I suspect, have taken to rustling to make it through tough times. Those Eastern markets tend to get a little unstable now and then. Of equal concern to me is the fact that some of this money has been poured into the coffers of political candidates. Although I'm a Republican, I make no excuse for some members of my party. The word out of the White House is run a clean election or Wyoming can forget Statehood."

Lifting a cigar out of the humidor on his desk, Judge Darett said, "How familiar are you with that Shoshone Basin country?"

"Been there once or twice," said Philby.

"You're probably aware that it's a hotbed of rustling activity."

"Not any more than other parts of the territory."

"Unfortunately, that's true," said the governor. "Marshal, we want you to head back there as soon as possible. I've little doubt that the men who want certain favors will be contacting you."

"And if they do?"

"Then give them enough rope to hang themselves. I'd caution you, however, about trying to make any arrests right away. Since this web of criminal activity could even take you to the territorial capital."

Now, in Rock Springs, the parting words of Governor Randall, about wanting a clean political campaign, were in Philby's thoughts, but the very nature of things out here dictated otherwise. Life in this territory was based on corruption and greed. First there'd been Judge Darett pointing him toward the Shoshone Basin. Then, in Cheyenne, there'd been his dealings with cattle baron Tyler Barnett. To these Republicans, a clean campaign seemed to mean getting rid of the Democratic candidate.

Out here Keno Lane's past was an open book. The fact that Lane had been a scout for the U.S. Fifth Cavalry meant little to Marshal Philby, nor did the fact that he was a rancher turned politician. Philby knew of the sudden death of Lane's first wife after she'd borne him a son, of Lane's remarrying, and of that second tragedy which had occurred when a band of renegade Indians had kidnapped the Lane's young son, Jed. All of the hard facts turned up in the background investigation he'd made of Keno Lane, the bar talk, spoke of an honest man. However, flipping the coin over revealed hired guns on Lane's payroll and his ranch's location near the infamous Outlaw Trail. Every so often, it had been reported to Marshal Philby, the Cole Malone gang surfaced in Lander, South Pass City, or Fort Washakie — towns situated in the basin — and shortly after there'd been some rustling activity. Could there be a connection between the Malone gang and Keno Lane's Rocking K spread? Coming erect, Philby strolled downstreet in search of the one man who could give him some of the answers he was seeking.

Oftentimes in the past, Sheriff Lee Waring, a tall, somber man who favored a black frock coat and stiff-brimmed hat, had been of considerable help to Philby and his deputy marshals. Now when the front door of the jail swung open to show Marshal Philby haloed in yellow light, Waring dropped his quill pen and said quietly, "Heard you were in town, Ezra."

Closing the door as he entered, Philby dragged a chair over to the desk. "Sorry I didn't check in before."

"Got your reasons, I suspect." Sheriff Waring ran a bony finger along his dark handlebar mustache. "You're not the only visitor I had tonight. Keno Lane's wife was here. Swore out a warrant for some waddy named Starlight ... Jed Starlight. Claimed he stole some of her horses."

"Give you a description?"

"Young, about twenty or so, blondhaired. Though Keno's been through here before, Ezra, this was the first time I laid eyes on his wife. Struck a chord of memory, she did."

Removing his hat, Philby set it on a corner of the desk as he sat down. "How's that?"

"Back a few years I had occasion to go down to Dodge City and pick up a prisoner. There was this trial going on—couple of bank robbers. Well, Ezra, I'd swear one of the spectators in that courtoom was Mrs. Lane. Looked a heap different then, the way she wore her hair and all, and a lot younger; but her eyes haven't changed."

"Are you sure about this, Lee?"

"Not totally. Back at Dodge City she seemed interested in one of the men standing trial. But like they say, Ezra, everybody's got a double some place or other."

"Could be that's it. This Starlight could be the reason Terrapin and his men arrived on the train. Mighty strange since they left Rawlins ahorseback."

"Terrapin's nobody to mess with. Damned fast on the

94

draw. And a strange sort too . . . just like the woman he works for."

"Tell me, Lee, just how did Mrs. Lane act when she came in here? Was she the vengeful ranch owner?"

"For certain she's a bossy type of woman. Too damned strong-willed for my liking. Strange that you should ask me that, Ezra. Matter of fact, Mrs. Lane had more than average harsh words for this Jed Starlight . . . almost as though she wanted him dead. Didn't say that in so many words, but it was there, her fear of this Starlight."

"What's your opinion of Keno Lane?"

"Winning the election?"

"Your assessment of the man."

"Painfully honest. Someone who's had more than his share of sorrow."

"You're speaking of what happened to his son."

"They never did find out if the boy got killed or not. As for Keno's wife, she's more or less the boss out to their ranch. Why this sudden interest in Keno Lane?"

"Tell me flat out, Lee, is the Rocking K mixed up in rustling?"

"Can't say yes or no. Lord knows you'll find rustlers most everyplace in these parts. If Keno was running the Rocking K I'd not hesitate to say he wouldn't tolerate stealing cattle."

But he isn't ramrodding the place, and that's what is troubling me, Lee." Rising, Philby put on his hat. "One more thing—have you cut sign of that Cole Malone bunch lately?"

"Been a spell since they've been around. They operate up north more, which is just dandy with me. Staying long?"

"Take it day by day. Much obliged for the information, Lee. Would appreciate hearing from you if that Malone bunch shows up."

Out in the street, Marshal Ezra Philby knew it was time he got a glimpse of Etta Montclair Lane, and he set out for the Great Western Hotel. He knew Keno Lane had married Etta back in Cheyenne. But where she'd come from before that was something he meant to find out... along with just why in tarnation a ranchwoman needed the services of a man like Terrapin.

8

Earlier in the evening a passing band of clouds had dropped rainwater on Rock Springs giving its residents some relief from the sultry heat. The parched earth had within minutes, absorbed most of the downpour, the lights from the town now being reflected from small puddles of water in alleys and in ruts left by the wheels of carts and carriages, while main street was still being drummed hard by the hoofs of passing horses.

As in Rawlins, fireworks were bursting in a clearing sky, the second such display Jed Starlight had ever seen. It was some kind of pagan ritual, Cree Bonner had told him once, man celebrating his dominion over ancient fears and gods, and commemorating great victories won. Tonight it was being done, Starlight figured, more to incite people into spending hard-earned cash at the business places than to help the causes of the political candidates.

Having camped just south of town last night, Jed had observed from a butte the things taking place that day, so he knew Terrapin and the other killers had come in on a train. Others had used the main roads, and Starlight's interest had been aroused by the appearance of Marshal Philby and his deputies. Upon viewing them through the lens of his field glass he reasoned they were lawmen, since men on the dodge didn't ride blooded horses, nor were they so neat. They'd been riding purposefully too, like starpackers closing in on their quarry.

"Yup," Jed murmured from where he lurked in the mouth of an alley opening onto the main street. "Out here civilization is but a step removed from the dark ages." The trio of cowpunchers clattering past on the boardwalk glanced Starlight's way, but never broke stride for he was dressed as they were—Stetson, leather vest over a work shirt, revolver thonged down at his hip.

That brief encounter back in Rawlins with Crystal Lane had aroused all kinds of memories during his ride over to Rock Springs. But Jed had pushed them aside long enough to head the horses he'd stolen up a trail used frequently by passing bands of Indians. All along Jed had had the notion that peculiar birthmark of his was a curse, something that set him apart from the pack. Now, much to his surprise, it had become a link to his past. This Jed Lane Crystal had taken him for, he had a birthmark too.

"Lane . . . Jed Lane?" He set eyes narrowed in concentration on the facade of the Great Western Hotel. Crystal would be there, and this time she'd give him answers to questions that had been troubling him

98

since childhood. He half-turned to go, hesitated to study those thronging the streets. Perhaps it would be best to leave the past as it was. Only then the bad dreams of what happened to him when he'd been staked out and left to die would never go away. And so Jed cut back through the valley, a young man thirsting to clear up the mystery of who he was, unaware that a warrant was out for his arrest.

Three fiddlers, a drummer, and a skinny gent all but invisible behind a big bass fiddle were boisterously playing the strains of a waltz in the grand ballroom of the Great Western Hotel. To Etta Lane's approving eyes the large room was packed with dancers and others standing or sitting along the walls. Her husband, Keno, was, at the moment, dancing with a woman Etta disapproved of, a hussy from Cheyenne named Amanda Delaplaine. But after all, Keno had told his wife, the Delaplaine woman had invested quite heavily in his campaign.

Damned woman's still a hussy, Etta thought, her eyes then going to where her daughter, Crystal, was engaged in conversation with a nattily dressed young man, the son of a wealthy merchant. Someone who'd make a proper husband for Crystal. On the train ride over from Rawlins, and during the few times she'd been alone with her daughter here in Rock Springs, Etta had noticed how withdrawn she'd seemed. At first Etta had just put it down to the usual problems confronting a girl coming onto womanhood, and the one time Etta had tried to find out what was wrong, Crystal had told her to mind her own business. Some-

99

how Etta had managed to stay her hand, but once they were back at the ranch, she meant to straighten out Crystal's thinking once and for all. Pouting and back-talk had no place in a political campaign. Suddenly she became aware that Crystal had left the ballroom.

The feeling that he was here in Rock Springs had come again to Crystal Lane, and this was what had caused her to leave the ballroom. Slipping along one of the back corridors, she turned a corner, then glanced around it to see if anyone was following her. She waited a couple of minutes, then hurried to a back door, which stood open, and passed through it.

Out behind the hotel, Crystal threaded her way around some piles of debris waiting to be carted away, her heart pounding louder now, for her woman's intuition told her Jed Starlight was close at hand. His sudden whistle made her blink before swinging about to see him ease out of the deep shadow made by a sloping back porch attached to another building.

"Jed? Are you all right?"

"That depends." He stepped close to her, let the scent of her perfume and what lay in those lovely hazel eyes touch his senses.

"It depends upon someone seeing you here. My mother signed a warrant for your arrest . . . for stealing some horses. Tell me that isn't true, Jed."

"For a fact, it's gospel."

"How did you manage to get those horses away from Terrapin and his men." She found herself reaching out to touch his arm.

"Terrapin's lucky that's all I did. Now, Crystal,

100

what's all this about a birthmark?"

"We can't talk here." Crystal slipped her hand into his, and then they hurried away from the hotel, down a quiet street. Turning a corner, Jed guided her around to the side of a livery stable, to where a water trough stood under a windmill. Small chunks of mud stuck to their shoes from when they'd veered closely around drying puddles of water. But they seemed unaware of this, or of the sounds of the railroad town, lost as they were in the awareness of one another.

Then, in a hushed voice, she began the telling of how Keno Lane's natural son had been taken by a band of marauding Indians.

"... and so he was never seen again. Since it happened so long ago, it almost seems as if it had never taken place. But ... but standing close to you like this, Jed, you have the same shape to your face as Keno ... some of his mannerisms. And I can remember Keno talking about that birthmark – saying it was shaped like the wings of an eagle. Oh, Jed Starlight, can you be my missing ... brother?"

"Don't rightly know," he responded, and what he said next slipped out before he could stop it. "Don't rightly feel like your brother either, Crystal."

Through misting eyes, Crystal said, "I just know you're Jed Lane. Can you remember anything of what happened that night ... the night those Indians came."

"Mostly riding, forever it seemed. Recollect seeing some big hills – buttes, I guess – and then ... coming on horseback along this river. I recollect that 'cause of the sound it made flowing kind of fast over rocks ... white water. There was only the one man with me then

101

. . . the others had disappeared."

"Then what happened?"

"Cree Bonner chanced along. Told of finding me staked out by that river. Told of finding a hunk of raw meat perched on my chest . . . of me being stark naked. Of some timber wolves closing in."

"Damn, these Indians can be so cruel."

"Weren't no Injun left me there, Crystal."

"I don't understand."

"It took me until my yonker years, sixteen or so, to figure out Injuns as a rule don't have beards. The man who left me to die had one . . . and a sightless eye."

"He was blind in one eye?"

"Had no eyeball but a piece of round glass in there, such as the one that adorns Terrapin's face."

"Terrapin?" Her face paled.

"Yup, your *segundo* out at the Rocking K ranch."

"Jed," she said with some difficulty, "if what you say is true, then my mother could be involved in this. But, why?"

"Dunno, Crystal." Staring at her face, turned somber by what he'd revealed, at her tear-rimmed eyes, he resisted the temptation to reach out and take her in his arms. The only woman he'd ever known was a Shoshone, but what he felt now—and forever, he was certain—for raven-haired Crystal Lane was just pure love.

A voice coming from behind Jed Starlight lashed out at him, as did the metallic clicking made by the hammer of a gun being cocked. "Nice and easy now, Starlight," said Sheriff Lee Waring. "You, Miss Lane, ease away from him. That's it, a little bit more, though. You, Starlight, hoist your right hand over your head, then use your left to unbuckle your gunbelt."

Jed Starlight pivoted slowly around as he worked with his left hand at his belt buckle. Then, without warning, there came the harsh bucking of a six-gun, and he flinched, expecting to take a leaden slug in his chest. But a look of surprise came to the face of the sheriff of Rock Springs, and with a sudden outcry of pain, he staggered toward Starlight, only to pitch forward and land heavily against the water trough. Again flame lanced from the darkness at Starlight, and he drew his own weapon while going into a wary crouch.

Pow! Pow!

He'd pinpointed those shots as coming from someone hidden in a pole corral, and he triggered off two quick ones in return. When a slug nicked his arm Starlight flopped to the ground. Then a cry of pain coming from the lips of Crystal brought him up and over to where she'd fallen. Leathering his revolver, he dropped to his knees and stared in disbelief at the blood staining the front of her dress.

"Jed ... I ..."

Gently he cradled her head in his arms. "You're hurt, bad. It's my fault ... all my fault ..."

"Back here!" The shout was followed by the sound of people converging on the livery stable. Starlight's only thought was to pick up Crystal Lane and take her to a doctor.

"No, Jed, get away ... while you can. They'll take care of ... me."

"I'll be back," he said grimly, and he left her there. He broke toward the corral and the deeper shadows surrounding it as slugs from several guns hammered the air around him. Then he disappeared, and his pursuers turned their attention to those who lay near the water trough.

Every stalking creature leaves its track, Starlight knew, and soon he found what he was seeking—boot imprints left by the ambusher. In places the corral ground was spongy, and the boot marks were deep and outlined as if set in plaster. Though both heels showed signs of wear, in each there was a distinctive star marking, and from the size of the prints Starlight determined the man was of average height but walked favoring his right leg. Then he was out of the corral and heading at a run toward his horse, ground-hitched behind a crumbling shed at the end of the next side street.

Chaotically his mind dwelt on those who'd meant everything to him.

Teal Eye, butchered at the hands of the Blackfeet . . . Cree Bonner, gone the same way . . . a good friend, Mel Longstreet, bushwhacked because of him . . . and now the woman who claimed he was her brother lying back there and maybe dying.

Coming to his horse, Starlight vaulted into the saddle and rode out at a fast canter. It would take time to organize a posse, and since there was no moon showing, they wouldn't start after him until first light. Some instinct brought him up north of Rock Springs, and even farther northward toward the Shoshone Basin.

"Next time we meet, Terrapin!" he shouted bitterly, "I'm lifting your scalplock!"

Now, in his wondering anguish over whether Crystal Lane was still alive, the tears came and he was not ashamed of them, for they seemed to release some of his doubts about his mysterious past, and about the fact that he truly was, as the woman he loved claimed, the son of Keno Lane.

9

The gunhand Terrapin shuffled the deck of cards again before setting them on the worn table top, and after they'd been cut by the man seated to his right, Terrapin dealt out another hand of five-card stud. Beyond the glare of lamplight beaming against the window, he could make out the vague outline of the Great Western Hotel. She was over there, Etta Montclair Lane, dancing in the grand ballroom, and maybe once in a while having dark thoughts—as Terrapin was—while rubbing elbows with those supporting Keno in his attempt to become governor of Wyoming. Maybe she belonged in that company, again maybe not, but for certain Terrapin knew the woman he worked for was pondering over the uncertain future of her *segundo*. Elementary reasoning told him Etta couldn't afford to keep him around much longer, not with what he knew.

"You in?"

Wordlessly Terrapin flipped a chip onto the gathering pile on the table, and began passing out pasteboards to those who hadn't folded while mulling over his next course of action. Could he trust any of the hands he bossed out at the Rocking K? Not a mother's son of them! If she hadn't done so already, Etta would soon think of having one of the hands try to take him out when the conditions were right. And there was her brother, Cole, who'd always had a hankering to match his draw with Terrapin's.

When the three cards he'd just dealt himself didn't give him another seven, Terrapin discarded his hand. Glancing past some other players seated at the next table, he settled his eyes upon a man standing alone at the front end of the bar. In that dark brown cutaway coat showing a lot of red velvet vest and dazzling white shirt, the stranger belonged in a place more elegant than Hogan's Rimrock bar. This was no gunhand looking to carve another notch in his barrel, but there was a certain cocky hardness about the stranger.

The passage of another hour found Terrapin grown weary of barely breaking even and of the complaints of another loser, from his sloppy appearance a merchant. Removing his hat, Terrapin scooped his remaining chips into it and then put it back on before ambling, with wary irritation, up to the bar in order to get a closer look at the gent with the fancy vest. The barkeep, knowing Terrapin had been favoring whiskey all evening, produced a bottle of that and a shot glass, and, at Terrapin's request, a cold stein of beer.

"You're awful damned rude, mister!"

Fancy vest responded with, "Just my way I reckon. I came a far piece to see you, Terrapin."

"That so?" he said, while his sighted eye snaked down to see just what kind of rig fancy vest was wearing. "Well, speak your piece."

"Maybe we could sidle back yonder where it's more

private. . . ."

"Now, you're not one of them kind?"

"I'm a happily married man."

"Next you're gonna tell me you play the organ at the old folks home every Sunday afternoon."

The next few words spoken by fancy vest were without banter, and audible only to Terrapin, who squinted thoughtfully before gesturing for the stranger to go ahead of him to a back table. Easing down across the table from the stranger, Terrapin studied the man further while sipping at his whiskey.

"Well, shall I go on?"

"Depends. Just what is your line of work?"

"I'm a range detective," the man said candidly.

"Them who work for the cattle barons."

"As I said, your cooperation in this matter could prove extremely profitable."

"Or it could mean me getting backshot."

"Believe me, Terrapin, we want you alive. There's a lot at stake here."

"The governorship, I reckon. Just what do you want to know about Mrs. Lane?"

"We have reason to believe she's the sister of the outlaw Cole Malone."

"If you could prove this, you sure as hell wouldn't have come after me," Terrapin muttered stonily.

"That's correct. So, Terrapin, we do need your help. You came to work for the Rocking K right after Etta and Keno Lane got married."

"Close to a year after that."

"Then you were there when Keno's son disappeared."

"Yup. That really took the starch out of Keno. So?"

"Just putting all of this together. Back a good many years Etta and her brother operated out of Oklahoma, Colorado. Unfortunately, the few witnesses to the crimes they committed are either dead or moved to other places. We have more or less a prima facie case against them. Which is complicated further by the fact that thanks to the statute of limitations the time to prosecute Etta and her brother has expired."

"In other words, you ain't got nothing on Etta but just what I tell you. Look, I hate to do business with people who won't tell me their names."

"I'm Art Jenner, from up Billings way."

"What'll it be next week?"

"Yes, it's an alias. But believe me, Terrapin, the money I'm offering you is the genuine article. I'll confide in you further by saying that the people I work for are going to ignore the statute of limitations in the case of Etta Lane. Bogus papers have already been drawn up seeking her arrest."

"Wouldn't it be simpler for you people to put all of this in the newspapers?"

Through a smile, fancy vest said, "Out here very few people trust the printed word. And out here, too, womanhood is sacred. As for Etta Lane, we know she's tougher than most men, and we also suspect she's been receiving stolen cattle from her outlaw brother, then changing the brands before shipping the cattle to Eastern markets. Keno Lane is the weak link. Once he finds out about his wife, Keno's deep sense of honor will cause him to give up his campaign for the governorship."

Gulping down some of the beer, Terrapin wiped the spillage away from his face and said derisively, "Seems you gents have everything pretty much cut and dried."

"Right now the people I work for have the money, the power—"

"And a damned ruthless way of using both."

"This is how empires are created, Terrapin."

109

"Just how much money are we talking about? And it better be a heap, considering you people stand to gain this whole territory."

"Shall we say, twenty thousand dollars?"

"Them be silver dollars?"

"That could be arranged."

"Then once I tell you what I know about Etta Lane I'm heading south."

"The deal is, Terrapin, we need you here to testify against Mrs. Lane."

"Dammit, Jenner, sticking around here could be injurious to my health." Displeasure flared out of Terrapin's eye when a Rocking K hand shouldered through the batwings. It was Woodley, and stepping faster than he normally did, his limp caused by a lot of cartilage floating around in his right knee.

"There's been a shooting," Woodley announced. "This kid, Starlight, killed the sheriff. Gunned down Etta's daughter. Got away, too."

"Jenner, I'd best get over to the hotel."

"What about my offer?"

"We'll just have to give it a rest for now," barked out Terrapin as he shoved himself up from the table. He brought Woodley out the back door and into the alley. "Just what the hell happened?"

"I was keeping an eye on Etta's daughter like you told me to. When she snuck out of the hotel, I followed. And there he was, a-waiting for her, the Starlight kid. Trailed them over to this livery stable. Figured if I could sneak up on them in that pole corral I could overhear what they was talking about. Only thing was, Terrapin, that damnfool of a sheriff had to show up."

"Then Starlight gunned the sheriff down?"

"Something like that," he said evasively.

110

"What do ya mean, something like that?" questioned Terrapin. "It was you gunned the sheriff down, Woodley. What the hell for?"

" 'Cause the sheriff had the drop on the kid. So what the hell, I figured if I killed the kid, the sheriff would have to take the blame."

"You're a lousy shot, Woodley. You killed the wrong man. And when the kid began firing back, you hit the girl too."

"No, Terrapin, honest Injun, it weren't like—"

Reaching out, Terrapin grabbed a hunk of greasy shirt front and didn't stop hammering the waddy with his hard right fist until Woodley dropped to his knees. Then he sank a boot in the man's belly and kicked him away. "Get the hell back to the ranch! I'll finish this later!"

As the waddy, Woodley, picked himself up and stumbled away, Terrapin sucked angry air into his lungs. Of all the things to happen. Though he had little use for Crystal, she was Etta's daughter, and therefore entitled to his protection. But what in tarnation was she doing with Jed Starlight? How had she come to meet the kid in the first place? Unless, as Etta had told him, Crystal had overhead them talking in that hotel suite back in Rawlins. If this were the case, she knew that Starlight was Keno Lane's blood kin, and she knew of Terrapin's involvement in that bogus Indian attack on the ranch. She probably even suspected that the Rocking K was involved in rustling.

Which brought him right back to Etta Lane. Sure, he could tell this range detective, Jenner, about Etta's shady past, even testify against the woman in court. Etta would simply retaliate by implicating him in everything that had happened, and maybe a lot more. He was in a no-win situation. But twenty thousand would sure buy him a lot of happiness down in Old Mexico. He wasn't about to turn down that deal. Somehow, Terrapin knew, there was a way out of this thorny underbrush, and with that hopeful thought he set out for the Great Western Hotel, hoping that Crystal Lane was dead.

10

The posse, composed of locals and thrill seekers, left
before dawn to the clatter of hoofs and squealing of
leather, in high hopes they'd capture Starlight before
midmorning.

And when the sun had started branding red-tinted
light into the tarred rooftops of Rock Springs, U.S.
Marshal Ezra Philby and his men were fanning out by
the livery stable in their search for further evidence in
the case of Jedekiah Starlight versus the People of
Territorial Wyoming. The crowd had rushed over there
just after the shooting, hindering their search and
trampling out footprints left by the duelists Starlight
and Waring. The sheriff, much to Philby's surprise,
had been backshot. Somehow this didn't fit the image
he'd formed of a young cowpoke gritty enough to steal
the horses of a bunch of hardcases.

Last night a leaden slug, still retaining its shape,

had been surgically removed from Sheriff Waring's body. Now, peering at the water trough next to the stable, Marshal Philby, a hand-rolled cigar wedged in one corner of his mouth, could see where a couple of other lead pellets had scoured wood. Fishing out his jackknife, he pulled out one of its blades and used it to gouge out the slugs. Unlike the one taken from Waring's body these were flattened out and showed no rifling. Then one of his deputy marshals, J. D. Murdock, called to him from inside the pole corral.

"Found another slug in this post, Ezra."

"Same caliber?"

"Battered some, but from its heft I figure it came from a .36 caliber weapon, say a Navy Colt."

Philby beckoned all of his men over to have them congregate at the windmill. "Well, about all we have to go on are these slugs. Let's reconstruct what we believe happened here. You said, Rufus, that Starlight was spotted by the water trough. . . ."

"Got here just after them shots were fired," said Owsley, "to find Starlight"—he nodded to his left—"tending to the girl."

"Sheriff Waring's body was found sort of half in the trough. The impact of the bullet that hit him from behind had driven him forward—meaning the killer had to be back there someplace; maybe in that corral. Now, Waring's weapon, a Classic Peacemaker .45, had never been fired; though he'd been holding it." Philby held the cigar in his hand now.

"So this .36 caliber slug," said Murdock, "could mean there was a third gunman."

"The girl could tell us what took place," Philby said, "but she's still in a coma. Nevertheless, gentlemen, this could mean that Starlight didn't kill the sheriff." He passed the lead slugs to Owsley. "Head over to the assay office and have them weighed."

"I reckon, Ezra," Deputy Marshal Murdock put in, "that posse is so set on bloodletting they won't let Starlight give his version of what took place here."

Around his cigar the marshal said, "That is . . . if they catch Starlight."

Nodding, Murdock asked, "Do you still want us to keep track of Terrapin and his bunch?"

"For now, yes. J. D., hold up a minute." As the other deputy marshals walked away, Philby dragged on his cigar while studying the sky. The gathering clouds to the southwest told him it would probably rain later that day, and it would be hot again, hotter than yesterday. He moved with Murdock into the shadow cast by the back wall of the livery stable. "We know that Keno Lane has been spending pretty lavishly on his campaign."

"Probably getting some sizable campaign contributions."

"That could be. But he does have quite a payroll out at that ranch of his. We know he does his banking at Lander." Philby threw a courteous nod to a horseman drawing up by the stable. "I want you to go up there and check out his account; go back at least five years. Do the same at other towns in the basin."

"You saying, Ezra, some of Lane's money came from rustling."

"Exactly that. Simply because of those gunhands on his payroll."

Removing his hat, Murdock ran a hand around the inner band. "I had occasion to converse with Keno. Not a bad sort. Seems out of character that a man with his reputation would let this happen – rustling, I mean. Overheard others say Keno isn't the same man he was before his son up and disappeared. If his son Jed was alive today he'd be a big strapping blond just like his pa."

"J. D., I believe your suspicions match mine."

"About this Starlight kid maybe being Keno's long-lost son?"

"Could be one of the reasons Terrapin tried to kill Starlight. But who ordered it? Hard reckoning tells me its someone who stands to gain Keno Lane's holdings after he's gone."

"I'll bet Keno's will leaves everything to his wife."

"Yup, to dear Etta. Got a good look at dear Etta at that dance last night. Pretty woman, that is until you see her eyes. Sent chills up my backside, I tell you. Another puzzler is where Jed Starlight has been all these years."

"For certain he knows tracking. With some Indians, I'll wager."

"For certain. Anyway, all this jawing is just more speculation. J. D., get your gear together and head for Lander. We'll trail up thataway behind Terrapin's bunch."

The room they were in smelled of chloroform and disinfectant and it had white, sterile walls. A black leather couch stood next to a bookcase filled with medical books, but on one shelf space had been made for a human skull. The bowl of a briar pipe was sticking out of one of its eye sockets. On the opposite wall a framed certificate announced that Dr. Wilbur Jamison had graduated with honors from the Syracuse University Medical School. Marshal Ezra Philby was

116

used to rooms such as this, but he could tell that Keno Lane wanted to be elsewhere.

Without preamble the marshal said, "What was your daughter doing by that stable with Jed Starlight?"

"First off, Crystal is Etta's daughter," Keno said without malice. "And Marshal Philby, the name Starlight is unknown to me."

"It is claimed Starlight killed Sheriff Waring."

"So I've heard. Perhaps Crystal met this ... this Starlight at the dance last night. I must explain that we've never been close, although the girl means a lot to me."

"How is she?"

"Barring complications she'll pull through."

In the brief time he'd been here Philby had formed the firm opinion that Keno never laid eyes on Jed Starlight before, and he'd decided the man knew very little of what had been happening out at the Rocking K. Here was an honest Westerner, forged by the tragedies of his past; a man uncertain about his future even though he was running for governor. The stories were true, then, about Keno spending most of his time at the saloons and gambling halls while Etta, dear Etta, ran the ranch. This was not the time, Philby mused, to tell Keno that perhaps Jed Starlight could be his son. But Etta Montclair Lane knew all right, as did her daughter. Once he received a response to that wire he'd sent to Cheyenne requesting information on dear Etta a lot of his questions would be answered.

There was little doubt in his mind that Crystal Lane's life could still be in jeopardy because of her association with a young man someone wanted dead, and Philby voiced this to the rancher.

"You can't be serious?"

117

"I am, sir," Philby replied.

"But, why?"

"Because she knows Starlight's true identity."

"Well, just who is this mysterious Starlight—"

"I'd just be guessing, Keno."

Then the door opening onto the street stirred into motion and Etta Lane came into the room followed by her son, Darby. Casting the marshal a cold glance, she said to Keno, "Has she come out of that coma yet?"

"No change, Etta."

Marshal Philby detected her slight sigh of relief, and he stowed this away for future reference.

"Keno dear"—Etta reached up and touched her husband's stubbled face—"you'd better go back to the hotel and get some sleep. A lot of people have been asking about you. Oh, some telegrams of support are up in our suite." She looked the marshal's way. "Aren't you a lawman?"

"U.S. Marshal Ezra Philby at your service, ma'am."

"Shouldn't you be out looking for that dastardly killer!"

"There is a possibility Starlight is innocent," Philby said flatly.

"Whatever do you mean? That . . . monster shot my daughter."

"That monster, as you call him, is probably dead by now. Meaning that posse has captured Starlight and left him dangling from a tree." He tipped his hat to Etta Lane. "Keno, I'll talk to you later."

Striding outside, he moved along the gravely side street and bit the tip from a cigar, a bitter expression on his face. "There is one evil woman." He lit the cigar, inhaled thoughtfully. He suspected that Keno didn't love his wife anymore, that habit bound him to Etta.

The man seemed blinded by the past. Sooner or later Keno would open his mind's eye, only then it might be too late—for himself and for Crystal and the Starlight kid.

11

This is no country to get careless in.

Many a time Cree Bonner had drummed those words into Starlight, and there'd even been a time when the mountain man had leathered his breeches, this after a close call with a grizzly. So Jed had hidden his trail with an instilled cautiousness ever since leaving Rock Springs. Even though Granite Peak in the Wind River range beckoned to him, and he knew the posse had given up around high noon and turned back, Jed kept from being skylined, and his probing eyes were always looking for signs of movement, ahead or behind.

The cut in the mountains ahead was South Pass, and it took Starlight the rest of the day to traverse its rocky height. Coming off it, he got his first glimpse of South Pass City, while beyond, the vast Shoshone Basin beckoned.

As Jed rode along the lowering track, he studied with distaste the jerry-built structures he was approaching, the tents and flimsy, wooden frame buildings put up on level tracts of ground, the empty liquor bottles and the other debris littering the track just turning into a wider road running toward a few false-fronted buildings. Those Indian villages he'd been in seemed like crystal palaces compared to this town. Life was cheap in places like this and scum was plentiful. Starlight's intention was to tarry just long enough to replenish his supplies and tend to his horse.

Draped over his lean frame was the working gear of a cowhand, and in one spurred boot, as a precautionary measure he'd hidden his Green River knife. After what had happened at Rock Springs, and before that in Rawlins, he could well believe Etta Lane was putting out a reader on him. Only now the charge of murder would be added to it. And besides, that big hunk of steel looked out of place hanging at his midriff. It would draw the eyes of those he was trying to evade. A painful memory came to him, of knife-throwing contests with Cree Bonner. They'd ended when he'd begun to take Bonner's measure pretty regular.

During the hard ride Jed had tried—and failed—to keep from thinking about Crystal Lane. He'd regretted his decision not to take her to a doctor, even though it would have meant his arrest and sure conviction. She had to be alive. She knew of his past. Along with that, she'd stolen his heart. Somehow he would have to construct a wall of granite around it, become immune to human suffering as Terrapin sure as sin was. For if he didn't, Jed realized these distracting thoughts could get him gunned down.

Just past a derrick pumping oil, Starlight reined his mount toward a large tent, the sign hanging from a post out front telling passers-by it traded in dry goods and groceries. He dismounted as two men emerged from the tent store, carrying gunny sacks and so grimy that at first Starlight took them to be Mexicans. As he tied the reins to the hitching post, Jed gazed downstreet at a tented saloon, and to other shelters showing light. Mel Longstreet had told him about another town such as this, Tombstone down in Arizona Territory, where there was so much violence the brag was that a dead man was served for breakfast every morning.

Inside the store he told the clerk behind the counter—a plank resting on two kegs—what he wanted in the way of possibles. Then he paid his bill in coin and, slinging the saddlebags over his shoulders, strode back to his horse. Only to be stopped just short of the hitching post by three armed men.

"Mister," said the one with a star and crescent badge pinned to his coat, "just where did you steal that horse?" Warily the man eased away from the tent while his companions, both holding Greeners, fanned to cover Starlight.

"I paid for that horse legal-like."

"That must mean you have a bill of sale—"

"No. I ... I ... plumb threw it away ..."

A pleased smile poking through a mass of scraggly black beard revealed some yellowed teeth. "That reader said to be on the lookout for a man astride a Slash L horse. A young, blond-haired gent. Which is you, Starlight! Makes no difference we take you in dead or alive."

Starlight complied by raising his hands high; then something clubbed into the side of his head and he dropped heavily to the ground. The man who'd just hit Starlight gazed with some concern at his sawn-off shotgun. "Hope I didn't crack the stock."

"If you did," said the man wearing the badge, "It'll damn sure come out of your wages."

"Can I keep his revolver, Sheriff?"

"Guess he won't be needing it no more. Especially

when Terrapin gets here and takes this hoss thief off'n my hands. But the horse is mine — that is, it's now the property of South Pass City. You boys get him over to the jail. Then I'm springing for drinks over at the Eagle Brewery." Holstering his revolver, Sheriff Ike Clark sauntered downstreet.

"I don't feel up to carrying no hunk of dead meat."

"Me neither. There's a lariat hanging from his saddle." The deputy stepped over to the horse and removed the lariat, and while his companion climbed into the saddle, he looped the rope around Starlight's legs, then tossed the rope up to the mounted man who looped it around the saddle horn. At a canter he dragged his prisoner along the rough pebble-strewn street, and from there along a dirt track, finally drawing rein before a barnlike building set off by itself. When the other deputy rode up, they carried Starlight into the building and tossed him on the cold dirt floor of a small back room. Locking the door, the deputies then set out for the saloon.

Sheriff Ike Clark had set up his office at a table in the Eagle Brewery saloon, and it was here that a messenger from the telegraph office found him. "Been looking for you, Ike." He passed a folded piece of paper to Clark. "Sheriff Waring down at Rock Springs got hisself killed."

Squinting at the telegram, the sheriff said, "Ain't this just peaches and cream. Now this Starlight's wanted for murder." He tossed the messenger two silver dollars. "Harold, one's for keeping your mouth shut about this wire; the other's to pay for a wire I want sent down to Rock Springs, addressed to a gent named Terrapin."

"Ain't this Terrapin the bossman out at the Rocking

K?"

"Never you mind about that, Harold. Just tell Terrapin this . . ."

Alone, the sheriff of South Pass City smiled inwardly as he helped himself to some more whiskey. Hoss thiefs were a dime a dozen, as were piano players judging from the discordant notes tinkling out of a piano in the adjoining room. But murder was a different cut of prime beef. Along with keeping Jed Starlight's horse and rigging, the lawman Ike Clark expected those Rocking K people to come up with a lot more money.

It was so dark in the small room that Starlight figured he must be dead, but the racking pain that came with consciousness told him otherwise. He rolled onto his back and, when the dizzy spell had passed, eased a hand up to find blood matting the side of his head and staining his neck. His probing fingers revealed a small cut, some swelling. Flexing his arms and legs, Jed was grateful to find there were no broken bones, though he had a painful sore spot at his rib cage. That was a result of being dragged behind his horse.

"The knife!"

"Had they found it?"

Pushing up from the cold dirt floor, he strained to reach inside his right boot. When his hand came out grasping the Green River knife, a groggy smile touched his lips.

After his head had cleared more, and he'd regained some of his strength, he went to the door, found that it was made of sturdy oak covered on the outside with a thin sheeting of metal. He moved along the outer walls, probing with his knife for any weak boards. He knew all was not lost when beads of light seeped into the room through a wide joint. Quickly he set about carving away at the inch-thick planking, hewing out small chunks of wood and letting in more and more night light. When he'd hacked out a sizable opening, yet one still too small for him to escape through, he grasped one of the wall boards with both hands and pulled with what force he had left. The board seemed to give a little, and urged on by this, he gripped it and yanked again. There was crackling noise, then he stumbled backward, grasping wood in his hands.

Coming erect, he managed to squeeze his body sideways through the opening, and then Starlight was free. He dropped into some short grass growing around the building.

Never panic when you lose your gun, came the voice of the mountain man. But make darned sure, yonker, you get it back.

Starlight went at a shambling walk around the side of the building and then slipped back inside through its wide front doors to discover that he was alone. Several horses were stabled there, and he found a water bucket from which he drank eagerly, before he tended to the throbbing parts of his body. Along the back wall, as revealed to him by moonlight flowing through the open hayloft door, was a small stack of hay. That was where he'd be when those who'd captured him returned. First, though, Jed saw to his horse, checking the saddle strappings but leaving his saddlebags where they'd been dropped by one of his captors. With his Green River knife thrust in his belt, Starlight made himself comfortable in the hay pile, covering himself but leaving a little opening to see through. The virtues of patience had been driven into him a long time ago, and so he closed his eyes and catnapped, letting that untamed part of him keen its ears for the return of the man who'd struck him so cowardly. . . .

"That Ike Clark is sure some generous soul."

"Sending us back here ain't generous, dammit," grumbled the other deputy as he slammed the front doors shut, the scuffing of their boots on the hard dirt floor vibrating Starlight's way. The deputy struck a light to a match, lit the lantern dangling from a peg driven into one of the posts supporting the roof.

Having checked the heavy lock on the door of Starlight's cell, the other deputy came back to pick up the saddlebags before easing down onto an empty packing crate. Once settled, he reached around behind the crate and produced a bottle of whiskey. Tossing it to the other deputy, he unbuckled one of the saddlebags and pulled out a pair of moccasins and Jed Starlight's buckskin suit.

"Now, lookee here at this fancy rig. Be it Comanche?"

"You damned fool, Comanche hang out down in Texas and such parts. That's a Blackfoot rig or I just don't know the way of Injuns. You gonna try it on?"

"You got that gun," whined his companion. "Sure I'm gonna put on what rightfully belongs to me now. See that beadwork? Sure is fancy. And lookee here at them leather fringes dangling all over this jacket."

"That thing could be lice ridden, or worse."

"I do believe you're jealouos. Just wait'll them gals over to the Eagle Brewery saloon see me in this getup."

They were unaware of a shadow drifting away from the pile of hay, and then Starlight was there. Viciously, he struck the deputy who'd stolen his gun alongside the temple, while the other deputy's eyes became round as silver dollars.

"What the—" The stunned man dropped the buckskin suit. "How'd you get out of there?" He went for his holstered gun, only to have that Green River knife slice through lamplight and drive deeply into his right shoulder.

Leaping forward, Jed picked up the man's gun, said grimly, "I could have killed you for sure, scum." He chopped the gun butt down hard to crumple the deputy's hat, and as the man dropped at his feet, he reached down and yanked out his knife, then retrieved the buckskin suit and moccasins, and stuffed them into a saddlebag. Draping the saddlebags over his horse, Starlight claimed his gunbelt before walking the stallion outside.

He had little rancor toward, nor respect for, the men who'd arrested him since, as scum, they were merely acting in character. His hatred was reserved for Etta Lane and her hired killer, Terrapin. Their day of reckoning was coming, and even if it meant a kid named Starlight going under, that would be the way of it.

He climbed tiredly into the saddle, but rode brazenly down main street and eastward into the Shoshone Basin, toward what his destiny would bring.

12

"Where do you suppose they are?"

"I thought for sure they'd be at Hole-in-the-Wall."

"But they weren't."

"About the only option we've got left, Logan, is to head into that maze of mountains ahead."

"There's another option open to us," said Burt Logan. "Up and quitting and going into another line of work. But we won't, Hadley, and you know why? Our salvation is that Keno wins the election. Then with Etta and Terrapin pulling the strings it won't be no time a'tall before we're rich men."

"You paint too rosy a picture for me, Burt."

A week ago they'd left Rock Springs in their search for the Cole Malone gang. Hadley was older, in his late thirties, with a more serious bent of mind. More years ago than he cared to remember he'd ranched where western Kansas fringed onto Colorado, until drought and hard times had claimed both his wife and land. Scarcely had the wind-blistered sands covered his wife's grave than he'd turned his vengeful anger upon the banker who'd refused to renew a loan way past due. That holdup had netted him around three thousand dollars, and ever since he'd ridden the owlhoot trail. But he'd come to dread every dawning, for at night he dreamed of being gunned down and left for the vultures. Hadley knew the half-blood, Burt Logan, despite his darker nature, had nightmares too.

On their ride across the basin Hadley and the half-blood had contacted no one who gave them a hint as to Cole Malone's present whereabouts until they headed due west again and arrived at the settlement of Crowheart, which hugged the south bank of the Wind River, where the basin shouldered against the Owl Creek and Wind River Mountains. At Crowheart a French Canuck named Dupère, while standing behind the bar in his trading post, nodded northwesterly toward Washakie Needles.

"You sure?" the half-blood had asked.

"Only one way to find out," Dupère had shot back, the withered fingers of his crippled left hand closing around the double eagle.

The click of the half-blood's rifle when he levered a shell into the breech didn't have any meaning for the blue grouse cock strutting amongst coneflowers spangling a mountain meadow as it attempted to attract a mate. Sighting along the blued-steel barrel, Logan's first shot pierced the grouse's red throat sac and then found the ground beyond. Right after, he shot another grouse just taking wing. Then the two men camped nearby under ponderosa pines, the dark hump of Washakie Needles looming nearby.

"Generally when Cole takes to these mountains it's to hide some stolen cattle."

"He must be gettin' low on cash," said Logan. He turned the grouse cooking on a spit over the campfire. "I hear you hired on shortly after Keno's kid got killed."

"What about it?"

"I heard it wasn't Indians that done it . . ."

Hadley stared hard at the half-blood hunkering down across the flames. He hawked spittle at the fire, finally said, "Woodley told me what happened . . . that it was him and some other hands done it, that it was Terrapin who took care of the kid. At the time he told me, we was raisin' hell over at Fort Washakie . . . half-drunk. Later, when he sobered up — and realized what he'd said — Woodley walked around shadow-spooked for a spell, I'll tell you."

"It was the woman who put Terrapin up to doin' it."

"Mrs. Lane? How'd you figure that?"

"I just know. Just as I know come sunup and we head out again, we'll find Cole's bunch."

"Maybe. Maybe you're right about the woman too, about Mrs. Lane. She's sure got devil eyes."

Logan produced a whiskey bottle. "A drink'll make you forget them."

"Sometimes it takes a helluva lot more than liquor."

The following morning found the hardcases heading into a canyon above which the mountain, Washakie Needles, loomed against a cloudy sky. The red sandstone walls of the canyon formed a colorful backdrop for the broadleaf trees and willows and cottonwoods that flourished along its rock-strewn bottom. They could hear running water before Logan, who rode out front, saw a sparkling stream carving an erratic course downslope and eventually beyond the foothills. Brushing against their faces was cool, moisture-laden air caused by the currents of heavier, warmer air swirling down from above. Lining the creek, alongside which they dismounted to walk their horses, were verdant stands of alder, ash, willow.

The half-blood held up a warning hand when a bald-faced steer meandered out of thick underbrush and began to drink from the creek. Logan said, "It seems that French Canuck was right."

"Could just be a stray," Hadley said crossly. "We could take forever to find Cole, or get lost trying."

Glancing back, the half-blood cast Hadley a wicked grin. "In that case I'll be getting my money back plus some interest. Come on, they're here, all right."

In their labored climb up the canyon, the eyes of both men often went to the starling-sized dippers plunging into the watery torrent careening over and around boulders. Other birds took flight at their approach—Western tanagers, Bullock's orioles, painted redstarts—and hawks were pinpoints of movement just below the wispy clouds touching the snowy peak above them. On their slow progress upward they encountered more and more grazing cattle bearing different brands. This brought a smile to Hadley's face.

"Maybe that half-blood's right after all," he muttered, while taking a swipe at his sweating face with his shirt sleeve.

"Got the feeling we're being glassed."

"Just so them idjits of Cole's don't mistake us for lawmen."

"Up there's one of them."

Hadley's eyes lifted past Logan's pointing hand to an armed man who'd just appeared on a rocky point.

"Ain't that Pinder?"

"Appears to be."

"Thought he got killed up at Cody?"

"That was McCann."

As both men swung into the saddle, Logan waved at the sentry and spurred his horse, to bring it laboring onto a high mountain plateau. Here began the pine forest of Washakie Needles—ponderosas, Douglas firs, aspens—a place of lush grass spread over bouldery ground and a forest floor littered with cones and pine needles, and dappled with patches of sunlight.

"Glad to see you boys," said Pinder, a bony-thin man with scraggly hair hanging down from a shapeless hat. He was heavily armed. He held a rifle, and had two revolvers tucked into worn holsters. "I reckon this means we're back in business again." He told them how to find Cole Malone's camp, an old trapper's cabin.

When they broke out of the forest into a clearing, the men lounging near the cabin spread out warily, then settled down upon recognizing Hadley and the half-blood. The clothing of the five outlaws was worn, patched here and there, and their eyes constantly bobbed from the cards they held to the surrounding terrain, their game being played on a blanket spread on the ground.

Just as Logan started to ask if Cole Malone was there, the outlaw emerged from the cabin. In the darkened doorway, Logan glimpsed a woman's face before it was quickly withdrawn. The sun, coming out from behind a cloud, struck down through the covering pines and set Malone's coal black eyes to sparkling. They seemed to have no whites in them, just large black and unblinking pupils. His wind-scoured and seamed face revealed Malone's character and the hard life he'd led. The man's dark brown hair was thinning, while the top four buttons of his dirty-blue shirt were open, showing matted chest hair turning gray. Logan found it hard to believe he was brother to Etta Lane, and a couple of years younger, according to the other hands. The half-blood figured Malone had just been with the woman, since he wore no gun and his fly was unbuttoned. But that was Cole Malone, a Southern redneck who answered to no man, no law. Now when Logan inquired about the cattle grazing down in the canyon, Malone told him they'd been picked up as an afterthought when returning from a week's drunk over at Worland, to insure they had some pocket change when things got tough.

"Etta wants you to go at it again," Logan said.

"Seems politics ain't cheap," came Malone's soft Southern drawl. "How's Keno doing?"

"Holding his own." Logan reached for the makings. "Got any spots in mind?"

"Some. That Powder River area, maybe."

"Soon's Terrapin gets back to the ranch," Logan informed the outlaw, "he'll have his men start throwin' a herd together; say around five hundred head."

"You two just messenger boys?"

"Terrapin told us to stay with you, Cole. He figures on doing some hiring down at South Pass City."

"A lot of cowpunchers have taken to that oil game," said Malone. "Along about now some of them probably want to set a saddle again."

Lowering his voice, the half-blood outlined to Cole Malone the plan Terrapin had. "So with enough men we can hit several ranches at once, take what stock we get to hiding places you've used before. Then after the brands have been changed, send them with that Rocking K herd to a railhead."

"Sounds good. But why was that U.S. marshal at Rock Springs?"

"Don't worry, Cole, if that Philby shows up he's goin' down."

Nodding, Malone told his men to saddle their horses, that it was branding time. He swung back to Logan. "You and Hadley ever used a running iron before?"

"Weaned on the damned thing."

"Got about fifty head below in that canyon. They'll do to get out some of the kinks we've got from all this loafin' we've been doing lately."

The next couple of days found them bringing together cattle that had scattered throughout the canyon, and during this time the half-blood, Logan, had the uneasy feeling someone was watching them. But he kept from voicing this to the others. Once in a while, he knew, Arapaho or Cheyenne would hunt game in this mountainous region. Since there wasn't much law in the basin, and the last he'd seen of Marshal Philby had been back at Rock Springs, he managed to put his worry aside.

Less than a hundred yards away the eyes of Jedekiah Starlight followed the half-blood's mounted attempt to chase a steer out of thorny underbrush, a muttered curse or two coming his way.

Upon leaving South Pass City, Starlight had gone to Keno Lane's Rocking K spread and found its headquarters located where the Sweetwater River made that big bend southward toward the Green Mountains. He'd come across line shacks and waddies tending to scattered bunches of cattle. He'd even been brazen enough to ride into the ranch buildings to have a noon meal and some sparse conversation with one of the cooks. Though the rambling fieldstone main house looked vaguely familiar as did the whole layout, there wasn't any one feature that proved to be a memory jogger, and Starlight had left.

It was just plain luck that found him on an elevation when he spotted dust behind some riders. Scoping them, he placed the two horsemen as some of those involved in the killing of that Chinaman back at Rawlins. And from the way they were riding, these two men were in somewhat of a hurry. When they rode into Crowheart, Starlight had trailed in behind, to eavesdrop on the owner of the trading post when he told the hardcases where the outlaw gang could be hanging out.

Now Jed focused his field glass on the three men branding a steer under the shading branches of alders. Right away he'd determined these to be stolen cattle, but it still seemed out of sorts that someone as important as Keno Lane could resort to thievery. The talk around Rawlins about rancher Lane had been mostly good, except for a few bad-mouthing Republicans. It could be money problems, or as Jed suspected, that woman of Keno's was behind all of this.

So here he was, wanted by the law, and dodging both badge wearers and outlaws. And all because of that peculiar birthmark. Maybe he should just chuck all of this skulking around and give the Great Plains and its sin-ridden towns the high sign as Cree Bonner had done—vanish forever in the spiny backbone of the Rockies. But he couldn't, and he knew it.

"Crystal . . ." The gentle breeze caught the word he'd

135

uttered and carried it away.

Though he was troubled, Jed Starlight would find the man with the star markings on his boots, to clear his name and to exact revenge for what had happened to Crystal Lane.

13

With the buggy carrying Etta Montclair Lane out front along with two horsemen besides Terrapin, the cavalcade of Rocking K riders left the choking mouth of South Pass. Closing in on South Pass City, they found the air tinged with the sulphuric stink common to all oil towns. The streets were clogged with pedestrians and four- and six-span teams pulling heavy oil rig equipment.

The town, observed Terrapin, had grown considerably since his last visit of a month ago. He still didn't care for the place, this despite the presence of more houses of pleasure and gambling dens to help sate the carnal cravings of its residents, temporary or otherwise. Though the Eagle Brewery saloon would do to wash the trail dust out of his mouth.

The man driving Etta Lane's buggy swung his horses streetside, then clambered down to check their harnesses as Terrapin drifted close to talk to the ranchwoman. Etta said, "Make sure you hire enough men."

"About two dozen should do it."

"I want this rustling operation completed in one month."

"You worried about that U.S. marshal?"

"I am. Some of his men were snooping around our hotel."

"Election campaigns bring a lot of con artists and outlaws out of the woodwork. So I'm figurin' they was looking for other outlaws besides us."

"I will not have you talking to me like that," said Etta as her face hardened.

Cuttingly he said, "It's what we are. What we'll always be. Remember, Etta, it was you who wanted Keno's son out of the way. Just so your dear precious Darby would inherit the Rocking K. All these years I've done what you asked. Once Keno gets elected, I expect to be paid off. Then I'll be out of your way for good." He saw the skeptical glimmer in her eyes. "Then you can have the whole damned State of Wyoming. 'Cause you've poisoned it for me, Etta."

"Until then, Terrapin, I'll expect you to carry out my orders. Understood?"

"Reckon so, Mrs. Lane."

"Tell the men they've got one hour to slake their thirst. Then we'll be pulling out for the ranch."

"Was it wise, Etta, leavin' your daughter back there, with Keno tending to her, I mean?"

"She's still in that coma; might take a long time to come out of it. Under the circumstances I had no other choice. But Darby's there, too, don't forget."

"What's that supposed to mean?"

"Darby will be giving her some very special medication."

"I don't like the sound of that, Etta."

138

"Surely you don't believe I'd harm my own flesh and blood?"

"Suppose not," said Terrapin. But he knew differently. Etta was capable of anything, and it just could be that the next time he saw either Keno or Darby they'd tell him of Crystal's passing.

"What really worries me," said Etta, "is what'll happen when Keno lays eyes upon Jed Starlight. Keno'll know, dammit, he'll know!"

"Let's cross that river when we come to it. Hell, every bounty hunter and lawman in the territory is looking for the kid. He's dead meat." Backing his horse, Terrapin watched the buggy roll upstreet.

He still hadn't figured out his reasons for not telling Etta the Starlight kid was jailed here in South Pass City. Maybe he enjoyed having her worried and strung out? Or was it to keep her from becoming a murderer? Then again, it could be he wanted to pay the kid back for stealing his horse. It would be interesting to see that winglike birth mark again, taunt the kid by telling him he'd changed his diapers back along the Wind River—then blow the lights out of Starlight's blue eyes.

It was said of the hardcase Terrapin, but never to his face, that he had no human compassion. The fact is, the hardcase didn't give a hoot in hell what anybody thought about him. And that included Etta Lane. Obviously, she'd duped a Rock Springs druggist into selling her some arsenic or rat poison, mixed it in with the medication being taken by her ailing daughter.

"Human compassion," snorted Terrapin. "I figure I've got more warmth in my glass eye than Etta's got in her whole body."

He brought his horse along the street and left it standing out front of the Eagle Brewery, where some

139

of the other hands had congregated as they debated over which saloon to go in.

"You boys have got one hour. So I'd suggest you quit jawin' and start gettin' what drinks you can under your belts. 'Cause it'll be a month's dry spell before you see a bar again." They scattered at Terrapin's words. What passed for a smile wedged space between his thin lips. Once Starlight was out of the way, he could turn his attention to hiring some men who weren't too particular about what they did, then head them over to Crowheart for that get-together with Cole Malone. Then he'd go back to the business of ramrodding the Rocking K.

The saloon was crowded, with smoke and conversation brushing the ceiling, and it took a moment for Terrapin to find the sheriff of South Pass City holding court at a table resting under a wagon wheel that dangled from the ceiling, four lanterns attached to it. Sheriff Ike Clark was dealing himself a game of solitaire while engaged in conversation with two gents wearing somber suits. But the talk came to a sudden conclusion when the sheriff saw Terrapin heading toward his table.

"Reverend Nelson, we'll discuss the devil and his ways later . . ."

"But I insist, Sheriff Clark, you consider Sunday closing."

"I do that and South Pass City will have another lynching. Now, why don't you and the deacon here trot over to the church and let the devil out?"

"Why, sir, that's . . . that's blasphemy . . ." Huffing angry air into his lungs, the minister took his departure.

As Terrapin eased onto a chair, the sheriff told one of the barkeeps to bring another shot glass over to his table. Placing the deck of cards aside, Ike Clark waited until the hardcase had downed a couple shots of whiskey, and then he said, "Well, we caught this Starlight all right."

"Meaning?"

"Didn't figure a kid like that to have a hold-out knife. He got away, Terrapin."

Grunting his displeasure, Terrapin drummed his fingers on the table as he sorted out his thoughts. By heading this way, the Starlight kid had made it plain there'd be trouble. He'd heard of how certain winged and earth critters could always find the way back to the place of their birth. For certain the kid would scout out the ranch. But this was Etta's worry now. Through slitted eyes he said, "You ever consider going into another line of work, Clark?"

"Many a time."

"Then do it." He helped himself to some more whiskey. "But you owe me one first. I want you to put out the word I'm lookin' to hire a couple of dozen gunhands. Tell them I'll be over at the Calumet Hotel." Shoving up from the table, Terrapin left the saloon.

He gave a bustled woman the eye, and stepping out into the street, began crossing over, only to pause when he noticed the man perched on a bench under the boardwalk. He veered that way and stepped up on the worn planking. "You sure are a persistent cuss."

"Followed you over here from Rock Springs," said Art Jenner. "That offer is still open."

Terrapin propped a boot on the bench and stared hard at the range detective. "It ain't as simple as it sounds, Jenner. The catch in all of this is in me stickin' around after I've told what I know about Etta Lane."

"You'll be in protective custody."

"You mean behind bars, dammit!"

141

"I have been instructed to raise our offer to thirty thousand dollars, Terrapin. A tidy retirement fund when you reach Old Mexico."

"If'n I reach Old Mexico," he said derisively.

"Up on South Pass I had occasion to notice a bunch of horsemen heading this way. Know for a fact, Terrapin, it was U.S. Marshal Ezra Philby, and know that the marshal is keenly interested in what's happening out at the Rocking K."

"That's mighty dangerous talk, Jenner." Terrapin brought his boot jarringly to the boardwalk and eased his coat flap away from his holstered revolver.

"These are facts," said an unruffled Art Jenner. "The way I see it you have no other choice but to help us out."

"Damn you, man, I hate to be told what to do. I'll mull this over tonight." By rights, raged Terrapin, I should call the range detective out right now.

"Sorry I riled you up," the man said softly as he stood up. "No offense meant, you understand. But politics is a very dirty game. Keno Lane's in over his head. I'll be around." The range detective headed for a saloon.

As he closed on the Calumet Hotel, Terrapin pushed his anger away. He realized that matters were coming to a head in the Shoshone Basin. Even if they managed to kill that U.S. marshal and his men, it wouldn't keep others from coming out here. Terrapin had seen what money and power had done for Etta Lane, and in him was a craving to have a share of both. He'd take that range detective up on his offer, but only after the Rocking K herd and the cattle stolen by the Cole Malone gang had been driven up to Sheridan. Instead of depositing the money a buyer would give him for the cattle in a Sheridan bank, Terrapin would deposit the money in his saddlebags when he headed south. Then let Etta stew in her own sins, and in poverty, for she'd soon lose everything—the Rocking K, Keno Lane, and her dreams of living in the state capital at Cheyenne.

14

Since the bullet had pierced her body and they'd brought Crystal Lane to this suite in the Great Western Hotel the steady ticktocking of the clock resting on the dresser in her room, the nearby murmur of voices and the creaking of floorboards, the sounds of the townspeople of Rock Springs, these had been her only communication with the world.

The doctor had said she was in a coma, but even in this unconscious state, Crystal Lane could understand but not react to those speaking to her. Every passing day brought an easing of the pain from her wound, and a release of mind had come with Etta Lane's departure.

Three days ago, or so it seemed to Crystal, her mother had come in on silent feet to slip onto a chair by the bed. At first she'd stroked Crystal's arm and forehead, and then the words had come, guttural sounding and terrifying in their impact upon the young Crystal.

"I know why you were with Starlight," Etta Lane

had said, her hate-glittering eyes focused on her daughter's composed features. "You know—don't you, Crystal dear?—that he's Keno's son, Jed. However did you find out? But that doesn't matter now. If only Terrapin had done the job right, killed Jed back then, you wouldn't be lying here now. But that doesn't matter either, my child. You see, Crystal, your brother Darby is going to be the instrument of your death. Only he'll be unaware of that. Let's just say, my child, the love potion I gave Darby will soon bring about your passing. But don't worry, my darling daughter, yours will be almost a painless death."

Then Etta had gone, leaving her daughter in a state of inner turmoil. Inwardly, tears had come to Crystal, the horrifying words of her mother still ringing in her mind. She hadn't been blinded to the crooked business happening out at the ranch. She knew brands as well as any hand, could detect on cattle supposedly belonging to the Rocking K the slight alteration of brand markings. What she hadn't realized until now that her mother was a very dangerous and heartless woman? Only one crazed could kill her own daughter, and get involved with men like Terrapin.

The door to her bedroom creaked open, and from the light football coming toward her bed she knew it was her brother Darby with that bitter-tasting medicine he'd been giving her. Every time she'd taken the medicine Crystal had suffered from stomach cramps, a weakness spreading throughout her body.

"It's me, Crystal," murmured Darby Lane. Dark-haired as his mother was, he had an angular face firming into manhood. He was eighteen, someone who'd rather read a book than do ranch work.

Her head propped on the fluffy down pillow, Crystal strained desperately to open her eyes, to make Darby aware that she mustn't take any more of Etta's love potion. One finger moved, and there was a tightening of the muscles around her mouth, so when Darby brought the spoon toward her face, it was to find Crystal resisting his efforts to give her the medicine.

"Crystal, can you hear me?" He lowered the spoon. "If you're to get well you must take this."

Only the ticking clock answered Darby Lane. With a pensive smile for his sister, he poured the medicine back into the bottle and capped it. "Sis ... I'm worried about you. Etta's gone back to the ranch, and me and Keno have been tending to you. But I know you'll be all right ... soon. I brought along some books. Wouldn't mind reading to you." Saying that, he adjusted the wick of the lamp on the nightstand and sat down.

"Now, yesterday I read where Tom Sawyer and Huck Finn got themselves this raft ..."

He read that chapter, and amid the whisper of a page turning, another. Then shadows started drifting in the eastern windows to trail across the big circular rug on the floor. Chancing to glance up from the book, he recoiled backward when he noticed Crystal staring at him in a dreamy sort of way.

"You ... you ... can you hear me ..." The book fell to the floor and he quickly sat beside her on the bed.

Weakly she reached out to touch him. "Dar-Darby, I heard every word you .... said to me. Keno?"

"Oh, gee, gosh, sis," he blurted out. "This means you're gonna live!"

"Must talk to Keno."

"You betcha! You ... you won't go away now?" Throwing her a smile, Darby bolted out of the room.

With the cessation of the political campaign in Rock Springs, there was a lessening of its populace. So when Darby Lane didn't find Keno downstairs in the hotel, he knew the rancher would probably be at one of the saloons or gambling dens, and if not at one of these places, he'd be with that woman who'd been supporting his campaign. His inquiries along the street brought the surprising response that Keno Lane had gone over to the church, a big whitewashed building surrounded by elm trees and set off by itself. Upon going there at a run, he encountered the rancher just coming out the front door.

"It's Crystal!" he yelled. "She's come out of it, Keno! She's gonna be all right!" The youngster pranced around the rancher in a leaping dance of joy.

"That's wonderful, boy," responded Keno as he draped an arm around Darby's shoulders, and together they hurried back down the dusty lane. "Just wonderful." Briefly, he wondered how Etta would take the news. It seemed strange that she'd been in such an awful hurry to return home, that the ranch was more important than Crystal.

And stranger still, when both of them entered Crystal's room, she insisted upon being alone with her stepfather, Keno. Noticing the glimmer of urgency in her eyes, he asked Darby to wait in the living room and, closing the door, came to sit by her.

"I feel better now," she said weakly. "Just being able to talk, to see, to know I'll live."

Grasping her hand, he said, "You sure mean a lot to me, Crystal."

"Not until lately did I know how I love you, Keno, for . . . for being such a wonderful father. But what I tell you next might hurt you terribly."

"It's about Etta, isn't it?"

Hesitantly she told of Etta's attempt to poison her, making it clear that Darby had only been carrying out his mother's orders. Then other thoughts came to mind, and Crystal spoke about things she'd noticed out at the ranch. As she did Keno Lane seemed to change right before her eyes, his handsome face firming, becoming flintier of eye.

"I know, Keno, how you've suffered all these years."

"Yup. Every so often I'd think about . . . Jed. But at least he's been with the angels—won't know that things have worsened between Etta and me."

"I was shot because of Jed."

"That doesn't make sense?"

"Before I tell you why, Keno, I must have your solemn promise you won't leave me behind. I must go back to the ranch with you. I must try to keep Jed Starlight from getting killed."

"Starlight? He's the man who shot you?"

"It wasn't Starlight who did this. And you know why, Keno?"

A questioning frown creased the rancher's forehead; and could that be a glimmer of hope in his eyes?

"I have reason to believe that Jed Starlight's your son! It's true, Keno. I know it. He's got your looks, eyes—"

"There's that birthmark."

"He's got that, too."

"Crystal," he cried out in disbelief, as a tear drop fell from his right eye, and then Keno Lane had swept her into his arms. "Suddenly I feel like a whole man again." She trembled in his arms, the salt of her tears mingling with his, and then he held her away.

Grains of thought started to form in his mind, cultivating them he came to Rawlins, and what had happened there. This Jed Starlight had been involved in a shooting at Rawlins, and now here in Rock Springs.

Crystal interrupted Keno's musings. "Back at that hotel in Rawlins I overheard Terrapin talking to Etta. Terrapin had been over at that sideshow and seen Starlight take on that professional boxer. Right off, up in that suite, he told Etta about Starlight having a birthmark just like Jed's, said Starlight could be your identical twin when he turned fifty. Then . . . then . . ."

"Go on, Crystal, please?"

"Etta said . . ." Paling, she pointed at the water glass, and picking it up, Keno brought it to her trembling lips. She gulped down a little water. "Etta said that she thought Terrapin had killed your son up on the Wind River."

"It wasn't Indians, then?" Keno said painfully. "She ordered it done! It doesn't make any sense."

"Knowing my mother it was because of her fears that you'd leave everything to Jed. There's something else, Keno."

"How in the hell could there be?" he said hotly, standing up.

"It seems I'm related to Cole Malone."

"That outlaw?"

"Cole is Etta's brother."

Wearily, he rubbed the nape of his neck. "That explains a lot of things. I . . . I kind of let go after Jed disappeared. Took to letting Etta run the ranch. And all this time I put my sudden prosperity out at the Rocking K down to her good management. All these years she's been involved in rustling. No wonder she headed back there. Simply to get some more cash together, which to Etta means having her outlaw brother rustle some more cattle. Yup, Crystal, all of these long, lonely years Etta thought she was doing this just to build up our name, to make us socially acceptable to the money men and their high-falutin' women. But all she's succeeded in doing was to drag my name into the dirt."

"Keno, I'm the only one who knows Jed didn't shoot me or the sheriff of Rock Springs."

"Which means I've got to find Jed, and quickly.

149

That'll mean leaving you behind, Crystal."

"I must be there," she cried out.

"Reckon so," he finally said. "I'll send Darby for the doctor. Meanwhile, I'll go see if that U.S. marshal is still hanging around town."

15

The Cole Malone gang had driven the stolen cattle into a box canyon and sealed off its mouth with brush, and had thereupon ridden away from Washakie Needles and down through the foothills. Along the way to Crowheart the talk among the hardcases was of what they intended doing with the money they'd get from the rustled cattle. Cole's woman was with them, bundled up in some of his old clothes. There'd be women for the others, too, when they got to Crowheart, unless Terrapin and the men he'd hired were already there. This notion brought the horsemen into a lope.

Trailing out of sight was Jed Starlight. Last night he'd ghosted up the canyon to slink past the outlaw standing guard and go on foot to the outlaw encampment. The unguarded talk of Malone's men had been of rustling and gambling and women, and of crimes done and men gunned down. They'd bared their fangs as wolves do when packed together. Eyes aglitter, they'd sat clustered by their campfire, prideful of their killing skills, but still wary of one another. They knew that if one of them got bullet creased while pulling a job, the others wouldn't draw rein to lend a helping hand; that was the harsh credo they lived by. Starlight had heard enough to know hard times and killing were about to befall the ranchers in the Shoshone Basin.

The basin was just a vast reach of prairie stretching southeasterly between various mountain ranges. With the sun about nooning, it baked the thin grayish soil over which Starlight rode at a walk. His mount, the Slash L bronc, picked its way around sweet cactus showing yellow flowers tinged with red, clumps of rabbit brush, and black and gray sagebrush. There were occasional patches of white grass and tufted fescues. Pronghorns stood warily in the hazy distance, almost invisible below lava rock buttes, with the moon hanging like a day star over the Owl Creeks. Jed could feel the wind picking up, as it often did out there early in the day, dying down again in the midafternoon.

When he could see Crowheart hugging the Wind River, Starlight found a game trail that carried him to an elevation, and from above, he viewed the outlaws and the town beyond. The tendril of smoke came from a blacksmith shop, which, along with the trading post and three log cabins, made up the town. There'd be no law in a place like this. But the man he sought, Terrapin, would be there, and come dusk, Starlight meant to mosey in for a closer look.

Easing his bronc down the trail onto prairie, he angled westward and then headed toward the Wind River, glinting invitingly not far off. Thirty-odd minutes later, he came upon the river. He dismounted in shade cast by a cottonwood, his eyes going to a speckled trout swimming close to the overhanging bank. It had been some time since Jed had tasted one of his favorite delicacies, but his first order of business was to shed the trail dust in the river.

The bronc, which Jed had ground-hitched, began switching around and gazing at the screening underbrush, and when it whickered, Jed realized too late, that he had company. Pivoting, he took a long stride toward his booted Winchester.

"Starlight, it would give me no pleasure to gun you down!"

Outlaws, he knew, would have shot first and spoken later. He yelled back. "Show yourself!"

At his words, out from the underbrush along both sides of the river came armed men. They closed in on Starlight, those opposite wading across the shallow waters. By the cut of their clothing and their general appearance, it struck Starlight these men could have something to do with the law, and if so, he was about to be arrested and carted off to some jail or hung.

One of them, deputy marshal J. D. Murdock, glanced at Starlight's rifle before searching through his saddlebags. He then proclaimed, "Ezra, he doesn't have any hide-out gun."

"You, of course," said U.S. Marshal Ezra Philby, "be Jedekiah Starlight."

"I be him."

"The reader out on you says you're wanted for stealing horses and murder. May I see your gun?"

"Do I have any choice in the matter?"

"None that I can see."

With his thumb and forefinger Starlight lifted out his Navy Colt, to have it grasped by the marshal. Thoughtfully, Philby spun the cylinder, looked from Starlight to his men. "Starlight, tell me about that shooting incident back at Rock Springs."

"You be the law?"

"I am that." Philby fished out his badge to have it wink in the sunlight. He leathered his revolver, but kept Starlight's.

"There is a young woman involved in this whose name I will not mention as it might damage her reputation. Is ... she still alive?"

"Last I heard Miss Crystal Lane would pull through. I trust that relieves your anxiety, Starlight?"

"It does, sir, it sure does. Well, I met her at that hotel—the Great Western. We went for a walk. Then she told me her mother had brought charges against me for stealing them horses."

"Just how did you manage to get away with them?"

"The eyes of Terrapin and his men were blinded by arrogance and conceit."

"And darkness, I gather."

Jed Starlight went on to tell of releasing the horses near a trail frequented by Indians. By doing so, he said perhaps he wasn't a hoss thief.

"Charges have been filed, you understand. And my sworn duty is to uphold the law."

"Terrapin had done me wrong! Him and his men gunned down a friend of mine. But it goes back further than that, Marshal, a heap of years. And ... and Crystal never had a chance. That sheriff was shot in the back."

"Know that, Starlight. Also know you didn't do it."

"I've got a bead on the man who did, though."

"In that case I'd appreciate you giving me his description."

"Didn't actually see him, Marshal. Right after all of this happened I hustled over to the corral by that livery stable, found his boot prints. Got star markings in each heel. Know for certain I'll come across them again."

Philby said flatly, "Not out here you won't. Not looking under every rock in the basin you won't. I suppose you're aware, Starlight, that every lawman in these parts will be wanting to collect the reward money put on you by that ranchwoman. At this juncture in time I cannot have one of my men escort you back to stand trial. As you said, Starlight, it was not your intention to steal those horses for profit."

"It was not, sir."

"But for revenge, Starlight," said Philby.

"Terrapin's men shot a friend of mine over at Rawlins. I'd say one of them was involved in that incident at Rock Springs."

"So here you are, son, traipsing through the basin in your search for a man with certain markings on his boots. Now we spotted you trailing after those outlaws. What's Cole got, some cattle hid around Washakie Needles? I know he has. But just a small bunch, I figure. I also figure Cole Malone to be meeting over to Crowheart with Terrapin. You know that, don't you, Starlight?"

"I didn't palaver with any of those outlaws!"

"You can track, son. You're damned good at it. Which tells me you got close enough to their camp to overhear their plans. That right?"

"Right as rain, Marshal. Reason I'm going to Crowheart is that Terrapin'll be there. I aim to gun him down."

"I can't arrest those hardcases for jawing about their intentions to rustle cattle no more'n I can keep you from heading into Crowheart to brace that hardcase." Stepping close, he shoved Starlight's revolver into its holster. "You have your liberty back, son. And maybe just a short time to enjoy it. So, kid, vamoose."

The lawman watched Jed Starlight until he'd vanished around a river bend. Then they stood there and eyed Marshal Philby who'd stepped over to stare down at the eddying waters.

By rights, the marshal pondered, Starlight should go after the one person who was responsible for most of the rustling that had taken place in these parts for the last few years, the woman who'd provided a safe haven for her brother, the outlaw Cole Malone. Even though her daughter lay near death back at Rock Springs, Etta Lane had taken leave of the place. Which could only mean, and the thought, bolstered what Starlight had just told him that once again blood would be shed here. But for now about all Philby could do was to warn the ranchers. Without any evidence, he couldn't ride into Crowheart and arrest the hardcases congregating there. He had no case against Etta Lane either.

By not arresting Starlight, Ezra Philby realized he had probably signed his death notice. He simply had had no other choice. In the storm clouds gathering over the Shoshone Basin the kid was a lightning rod that would attract the fire of those wanting him six feet under.

16

The unvarnished plank bar in Frenchy Dupère's trading post had gouged and scored into it marks of violence, knife slashes and some bullet holes. It had felt the hand of the Indian, the demanding fists of trappers and cowpokes. It had witnessed two murders; one in which Frenchy Dupère had defended himself by firing his Greener at a Cree gone drunk-berserk; the other, a showdown between two waddies working out at the K-C ranch—both wanted exclusive, albeit temporary, rights to the charms of a local whore. It had been here in Crowheart through lean years, and a few good ones. Now, with the arrival of these hard-eyed men, the old planken bar braced itself for another round of violence.

Wedged in one corner among some barrels, there mostly for his protection, sat a peg-legged fiddler. His gaping maw of a mouth spouted the drunken words of a popular song, his scrawny hands, hooked to the fiddle and bow, were a blur of movement. His main job was that of swamper and he cleaned furs brought in by trappers, but his eyes were sparkling reddish-bright in the hopes that the tin basin at his feet would resound to the clinking of coin. Vain hope, old music man, for the scabby crew hired by Terrapin was flat busted, while Cole Malone's bunch had never been known for their generosity.

One of those hired by Terrapin let out a raucous yell and spun, staggering, away from the bar and out the open doorway to find that night had tarred the settlement of Crowheart. His belly was full of booze and buffer meat, courtesy of the *segundo* Terrapin, and right now the hardcase would willingly follow the man who'd hired him into the bottomless pit and beyond. Come tomorrow, however, when suffering the agonies of a hangover, there'd be no more loyalty.

"Them whores is a-waitin'," he said manfully, then headed at a lurching walk toward one of the cabins perched above the moon-glistening waters of the Wind River. The frogs stopped croaking at his wobbling progress along ground turning muddy as it merged with the clayey bank, but he didn't notice or glimpse the moon as he closed on the cabin.

At one of the tables in the trading post sat Terrapin and the outlaw Cole Malone and his woman, her jaded eyes on the brown-paper map the men were gesturing at, her jaws grinding away at a mouthful of chestnuts. Big fat flys darted through the smoky haze to draw blood when they touched flesh, and occasionally there'd be the sound of glass breaking as an empty bottle was disposed of. The stench in the place was picking up along with the tempo of the drinking and cussing and bragging.

The map drawn by Terrapin was a crude relief showing most of the ranches in the basin, its main roads and trails, and the differing mountain ranges. He swatted a fly that had been working away at the back of his hand, and said, "Once we determine where their herds are summering, we'll move in. But as I've said, Cole, the trick is to divide and conquer."

"Seems simple the way you word it," Malone said skeptically. "But there's that U.S. marshal to worry about."

"What's he got, five deputies? No way they can cover several hundred square miles" — Terrapin jabbed at the map — "at the same time. Just keep the cattle you steal up in those mountain hideouts. Then I'll get word to you when the Rocking K herd is ready to head out to Sheridan."

Malone stared hard at the map. "Guess it'll work at that. Only problem is, that motley crew you hired could be more trouble'n their worth."

"Every man jack of them has worked cattle before. Once they get back in the saddle they'll prove it. I'll guarantee their bonafides." He gestured for the barkeep, Dupère, to fetch over another bottle of whiskey.

"Mighty noble of my sister springin' for all this booze. Just how is the saintly one?"

"Etta's as mean as ever, Cole."

"Then she's sufferin' no pangs." Malone smiled back and took a swipe at his nose with his sleeve, then sniffed. "The wages of sin don't come cheap."

"Meaning?"

"This mountain air ain't good for my ailments. Once Keno gets elected governor I'm sure Etta'll talk him into granting me a pardon."

"How about your men?"

"Then I'll collect the bounty money on them. A man's got to have some folding money when he turns honest."

"Now, Cole," chided Terrapin, "just what would you

do in the way of honest toil?"

"Well, reckon I heard white-collar crime is the coming thing. Could try my hand at stealing stocks and bonds and such."

"Guess you'll never change."

"Don't intend to. Larceny and robbin' is what keeps me alive, Terrapin. That, and women like this."

Enjoy it best you can, Terrapin mused grimly. He'd come here with killing on his mind. In the not too distant future, he knew with a fatalistic certainty Etta Lane would turn her brother on him. He couldn't take the chance of Cole outdrawing him in a showdown, though it was a notion he relished. There was that range detective's offer of more money than Terrapin had ever pocketed before, and lately his dreams of how he'd spend it. And there was the money he'd get for the Rocking K herd. But daydreams didn't get the job done.

In a thicket of willows edging upon the river, Jed Starlight's bronc nuzzled his shoulder. He was sitting on one of those bone-sheen tree trunks washed ashore a summer or so ago, with a clear view of the trading post. Jed had been witness to the hardcases making tracks to a couple of cabins just upstream. Also, he'd tallied thirty horses milling about in a pole corral, and though their owners were pretty much under the influence of liquor at the moment, the outlaws were still capable of sudden violence.

"Expect the worst when riding into an Indian encampment or a grizzly den," Jed cautioned himself. His teeth clamped on a dried strip of meat to yank away part of it, and patiently he chewed away as the night dragged on.

The moon larruping out from behind a peak in the

Rattlesnakes caused Starlight's sleep-drugged eyes to open. Stretching, he glanced at the trading post to discover Cole Malone and his scraggly-haired woman framed in a square patch of light, the woman trailing obediently behind like a Blackfoot squaw as Malone went over to one of the cabins.

Jed eased through willows and cottontails, came up the low bank to draw up short among thistle-bearing weeds when Terrapin left the trading post and vanished around a side wall. Having scouted the lay of the settlement from a nearby mesa, Starlight figured the hardcase could be heading for the lone cabin standing behind the trading post. Now light etched yellow against the paper-covered window in the cabin occupied by Cole Malone, and quickly Starlight eased out of this telling glow. Then the darkness thickened when the moon slipped behind another peak, the few buildings now resembling black ink spots on gray paper. Down by the pole corral to Jed's left, there was movement among the horses, followed by a drunken curse, the tittering laugh of one of the whores. Jed pressed on. While trying to plumb if anybody was lurking between the buildings he crossed the hard-packed lane passing in front of the trading post, and paused again when he detected a brief stir of movement.

"Cole!" came a voice. "Cole you dog, get out here!"

"That's Terrapin," uttered Jed Starlight.

Suddenly the cabin door was thrown open and Cole Malone lunged out, clad only in long johns and grasping a six-gun. Before he could frame a response, orange flame spiked the darkness. He took two slugs, one slicing an ear away, the second punching a nasty hole in his beer-stretched belly, and with a curse he fired back before stumbling sideways and smashing down against the log wall.

Malone's woman darted outside and screamed, "Terrapin . . . you killed my man!"

"Get back!" Starlight warned her as he dragged out his revolver while springing around the cabin in an attempt to shield the woman from what he sensed would happen next.

"Pow!" The ball fired by Terrapin drove the woman's pug nose back into her skull, and as she fell a little moan of pain and wonderment rattled out of her lips.

Another slug fired by Terrapin chipped wood near Starlight's head. And firing back, he whirled around even as men poured out of the trading post and the whoring cabins.

"Get him!" Terrapin yelled. "He done bushwhacked Cole and his woman! Get him, dammit!"

As darkness closed about him, one of Terrapin's slugs punched into Starlight's side, the hard impact tumbling him over, but regaining his feet, and somehow still gripping his weapon, he managed to slide down the embankment and find his bronc. Clawing his way into the saddle, he urged his bronc across the river and headed eastward at a gallop.

Somehow the French Canuck had found a Bible among his stock. It hadn't been opened for so long its dry, crinkling pages seemed to cringe away from the daylight just seeping over the eastern foothills. That book was now being held somewhat irreverently in the wind-scoured hands of Terrapin. A northwest wind tugged at the unkempt hair fluttering around his collar and blew dust over the twin mounds of sparse soil and rock on the little hillock some hundred rods north of Crowheart. Despite the expression of concern on Terrapin's face, his scar and mangy beard made him look more devil than preacher. The gusting wind had driven a speck of sand into his eye and in trying to work it out a teardrop had glistened onto his cheek, something noted by those hardcases who'd managed to pry their drunk-slitted eyes open. One of their own had gone under – a sobering fact that would be forgotten by nightfall.

"He was something, was Cole," Terrapin muttered bitterly. "You could always depend on him when times was tough. Like this here book says, according to what I've been told, since I've never browsed through one before, it's an eye for an eye. Snapping the Bible shut, he tossed it onto Cole Malone's final resting place.

"Cole was done in by a scurvy coward named Jed Starlight. We ain't gonna forget that. And it don't change our plans none about going after them cattle. Pinder, just last night Cole was telling me that if he cashed in his chips you'd be the one to take over his gang. You feel up to it!"

"I reckon I do," the outlaw said testily.

"You know where all the hideouts are."

A wolfish grin on his face, Pinder gestured with his hat toward the settlement. "Better'n I know that whore's backside." There was a little appreciative laughter. "A damned shame we don't head out after that backshootin' Starlight."

"No time for that now," said Terrapin. "All right, men, you had your fun last night. I told you how we're to work this. Three weeks from now, no more, I'm a-headin' the Rocking K herd uptrail toward Sheridan."

"Don't worry, Terrapin, we'll rustle us more cattle than you can handle."

"Hit them ranches hard and fast," Terrapin cautioned them. "Don't stick around to gather up any strays either. Kill when you have to. Something else. There'll be an extra two hundred silver dollars waitin' for every man jack of you up to Sheridan." He spat tobacco juice down at the graves. "As for you, Cole Malone, *adios.*"

163

Then he beckoned Burt Logan over.

Softly Logan said, "Pinder ain't been known to play with a full deck."

"Reason I want you riding with him, Burt. You and Hadley."

"He might not like it."

"Figure him to do something stupid. He does, kill him."

"Now that's something I'll like."

17

There was blood on Starlight's saddle, but drying now and attracting the fluttering attention of a dragonfly. Instinct had carried him away from the Wind River and up a dry wash onto tableland below Lizard Head peak and to a waterfall cascading down a worn rockface. Jed had plunged clothed into the rock-cradled pool at the base of the falls. Ever so slowly the chilling waters had eased the pain stitching at his side wound. His head had cleared, the anger over what had happened still there, his horse drifting over to feed upon a clump of sere grass.

Ducking his head under the surface, he came up gasping and spitting out water. He crawled out of the pool and slumped down on a flat rock and removed his upper garments. The bullet, he found, had passed through the shallow wound, the danger now that of it becoming infected, and Starlight set about building a fire, to collect the makings working his painful way among boulders and smooth-edged rocks forming the floor of the gorge. Except for the murmuring creek and his labored breathing a deep silence held sway even as fiery red darts were sparking the fringe of sky showing above the granite walls. He felt disjoined, confused, like a piece of flotsam being carried down a cascading stream during spring runoff. And he'd never felt more alone.

Killing scum such as Terrapin was a job that had to be done, like treating cattle for ticks or stamping out a smallpox epidemic. Etta Lane fit right in there too. It seemed strange that all of this had come about because of his fighting that professional boxer back at Rawlins.

It was destiny, Jed knew. There were no longer any puzzling doubt as to his true identity.

"You was right, Cree Bonner, that I might not like what I'd find."

Wistfully his eyes rose to a distant range of peaks being dusted with a new day's glow. There was home. There among the crags and plateaus and virgin forest. It's only voice that of the wind, the elk, the deer, and the silver-tufted grizzly. Even though his mind and limbs ached for the embrace of the wild, the heart of Jed Starlight had been given to a woman named Crystal. She was still alive, according to that U.S. marshal, and maybe he'd slipped out of her memory by now. But if this was love, Jed knew he had it bad. Along with a fierce yearning to confront his father, Keno Lane.

After the fire had caught, he unsheathed the Green River knife and held the blade close to the flames. When the tip glowed crimson he gazed down at the side wound.

"Here goes," said Jed through gritted teeth, and quickly he pressed the hot steel over the wound opening. Flesh seared as he gasped in pain, and he dropped to his knees. Almost blinded by the sting of his sweat, and steeling himself against the pounding waves of dizziness, he reheated the blade, mustered what courage he had left, and, with a trembling hand, brought the blade around to cauterize the exit wound. Then the knife slipped from his nerveless fingers and he toppled over.

After a while a dream came to him. Mystically that winglike birthmark had left his chest, its wings carrying him among mountainous peaks enshrouded in cloud. Spread out hazily below was the basin called Shoshone. Starlight knew this was a vision since he heard the beating of tom-toms, and saw, upon gazing far, far below at the plain, the tepee of a holy man, who was dancing around a blue-flamed campfire, and so Starlight flew that way. Strangely enough he knew the holy man to be a Shoshone named Red Elk. The Indian wore a robe decorated with religious symbols and a headdress made of eagle feathers, and he shook the rattle he was carrying at Jed Starlight and proclaimed:

"Our father, Wakan-Tanka, has made this known to me, son of Cree Bonner. There is great danger to the east. Where the evil woman lives. There you must go, Starlight. To your destiny . . . or to your death." Dancing close, Red Elk shook his rattle and sent rainwater spilling over Jed Starlight.

When Starlight finally came awake it was to discover that it was raining, and weakly he pushed to a sitting position. The bronc had drifted farther down the gorge, the fire having died out some time ago, and it was hazing into dusk. Retrieving the knife and hat, he struggled to his feet to stand swaying for a few moments. Then he moved stiffly downstream toward his grazing mount. The bronc shied at his approach, but luckily for Starlight made no attempt to bolt away. He climbed weakly into the saddle to the glimmer of sheet lightning and rode slowly down along the gorge.

The holy man of his dream hadn't faded away, and wryly Jed said, "I'll be heading that way, Red Elk. But I won't be reckless as before." And fearing what could happen if he rode along the creek bottom now that it was raining, he brought his horse to higher ground.

It would take some time, perhaps a week, Starlight determined, for that U.S. marshal to get word to all of the ranchers as to the rustling intentions of Terrapin and those outlaws. But that was Ezra Philby's problem. Starlight had his sights set on finding not only Terrapin but the man who'd wounded Crystal, and Jed's vision had told him both men were at Etta Lane's ranch. Somehow he couldn't tie Keno Lane in with that place, or even being married to his stepmother. After he got the drop on these men, he would have Keno confront both of them. Keno Lane must know the truth about his murdering wife, about her past misdeeds.

Jed's passage brought him out of the gorge and onto a plateau. The rain came down harder, not swirling about since there wasn't any wind, but colder now that night was approaching. Though drenched, he felt refreshed, and more clearheaded. Moving under a high canopy of Douglas firs, he went at a walk until coming upon a fallen tree, and it was here he pitched his camp, where only a few trickles of rainwater could penetrate. He gathered some dry wood to make a campfire. Hacking a branch away from the dead tree, he cut it into short lengths, cut the wet outer wood away and trimmed what remained down, featherlike, to form fuzz sticks which he used to start the fire. Jed listened to the hunger pangs gnawing at his stomach as he removed the saddlebags and unsaddled the bronc. Though game was plentiful in these parts, one shot by him could bring some unwelcome guests; so he settled down close to the fire to eat the rest of the dried beef and the remaining piece of hardtack. Some of the loneliness had gone away now that he'd treated his wound, and driven away a few self-pitying thoughts.

Like that holy man had said, you struck out after your destiny and worried about other things later. If a man didn't, Starlight knew, old Wakan-Tanka could get riled something fierce.

"Crystal Lane."

The name sounded right on his lips, so he let it lay there for a while, his mind framing things he'd say to her if ever they encountered one another again. Sixty feet above where Jed lay in his bedroll the roof of the forest began to rustle as a wind started to pick up, and soon the stalking creatures of the mountains would be out. That notion comforted Starlight. He felt secure here. And tugging the mantle of darkness a little closer, he drifted off to sleep.

18

Last night it had begun.

Out here at T. O. Byrum's Lazy Creek spread, and at a couple of other ranches some twenty miles farther east. The outlaws had gotten away with a little over a hundred head, along with killing one of Byrum's hands and winging another. Surveying the northwest route taken by the fleeing rustlers were Ezra Philby's deputy marshals, all mounted, even the rancher who was astride a dappled black. Said the rancher, "I know you warned me, Marshal Philby, this could happen. But I didn't think they'd hit so close to the buildings."

Philby's cigar had gone out, and he struck light to it, then said, "For sure they're getting damned arrogant. And I don't have enough men to head up into the mountains after them. So I'm gonna have them come to me. Here's what I want you to do, Mr. Byrum."

It took three days of steady riding to gather up the Lazy Creek herd and bring the cattle below the foothills along the Big Horn River where it cut southeasterly through the basin. Along with five Lazy Creek hands, standing night watch were a couple deputy marshals. Concealed below willows along the river were Marshal Philby and the rest of his men, and a dozen waddies he'd managed to borrow from other ranches. Two nights of waiting for something to happen had made the men restless.

One of the hands muttered, "Four hundred head of cattle should make a tempting target. But this basin covers a heap of territory, Marshal."

"Patience is about all we've got going for us, son."

"The marshal's right," spoke up rancher Byrum.

The ground along the riverbank still retained the heat of day, and it was in the air too, so there was no need for a warming fire. In the deeper shadows cast by cottonwoods their horses were strung along a picket line. Out on the silvery-gleaming waters a fish jumped, and was gone in about the time it would take a man to blink. The talk among these Westerners was subdued. Their senses were alert to the lowing of the cattle, and all were eager to avenge the death of that Lazy Creek hand. Over the years others had died at the hands of rustlers, while some of these men carried scars left by leaden slugs. For certain there'd be blood shed that night.

Ezra Philby hadn't revealed to these men the part Terrapin was playing in the rustling. Nor had he mentioned his encounter with Jed Starlight back around Crowheart. He doubted that any of these men would take the word of someone wanted for stealing horses and murder as was Starlight. But one of those rustlers mentioned by Starlight, either Burt Logan or Hadley or that outlaw Pinder, would tell of Terrapin's involvement or they'd be left dangling under one of those cottonwoods. Though he doubted that Keno Lane had a hand in this, Philby had little sympathy for him, political campaign or no. A man should tend to the home fires first; that was the marshal's firm opinion.

There came a thudding of hoofs, and then the willows parted when a rider swept in to come along the sandy riverbank. Rufus Owsley, one of Philby's deputies, swung to the ground. "Riders coming in; a dozen or so."

"How long before they'll be here?"

"Quarter hour at the most."

"Mount up," Philby called out. "We'll head up along the riverbank and try to head them off before they get to the cattle." Untying his horse from the picket line, the marshal clambered into his saddle and pointed his mount upriver, J. D. Murdock just ahead of him and T. O. Byrum's black alongside. "I appreciate your coming, Mr. Byrum," he said.

"Sick and tired of getting hit by rustlers. Now's our chance to get rid of this scummy lot for good."

With Murdock veering first up a cut in the bank, the other riders trailed behind and onto undulating prairie, where they spread out in a cavalry line, unsheathing their rifles as they did so. At a hand signal from Philby the horsemen reined up, to have Rufus Owsley tell them the rustlers would shortly be passing through a sparse grove of stunted trees standing on this side of a creek flowing to the west.

Within moments the clatter of hoofs on the rocky creek bottom could be heard, and now dark shadows came through the trees and into the open, riders gesturing excitedly at the grazing cattle, the rustlers unaware that other horsemen were loping their way.

"Do it!" rasped out Philby as he opened fire.

The combined firepower of their rifles sliced into the rustlers and their horses. Saddles were emptied and horses squealed in agony as they took leaden slugs. Even though three of the rustlers managed to break back into the trees and get away, it was over within minutes. Cautiously Philby brought his bunch up to those outlaws still alive, some still sitting in their saddles, others sprawled on the ground and clutching at their wounds, or dead. While his men set about disarming the rustlers, Philby eyed from his saddle the dead body of Burt Logan, and beyond that, Hadley. A rattling sigh was issuing from his lips as he stiffened into death. Dismounting, the marshal stared without pity at another outlaw who'd been wounded.

"I want some words with you, Pinder."

"I'm hit bad," moaned the outlaw, clutching at his upper leg.

"Who's behind this?"

"Behind what? Need a sawbones, bad, dammit."

At Marshal Philby's crisp order some of the men set about building a fire. This took around ten minutes, during which the marshal kept staring stony-eyed at the outlaw gasping in pain. After the fire had taken, he reached down and grabbed Pinder's coat collar at the back, then dragged the terrified man closer to the campfire. Taking out his pocket knife, Philby unclasped a blade to make a quick slash through Pinder's blue jeans from the upper thigh to the boot top.

"I want to know about Terrapin."

"Who the hell's he?"

Grasping the outlaw's right hand, Philby forced the knife handle into it, and said grimly, "Could be that slug pierced a main artery in which case you'll bleed to death . . . or you'll suffer lead poisoning by the time we get you to a sawbones. You've got a knife, Pinder, take that slug out."

"Me?" His already pale face went paler as he gaped at the blood still seeping from the ragged bullet hole. Then he flared his eyes over at the others staring down grimly at him, saw plain on the face of his captors their utter contempt and deep anger.

Choking back a sob, sweat beginning to pop out on his face, the outlaw turned to present his thigh to the light, and, gasping, he opened the mouth of the wound to let it bleed freely. Tentatively the fingers of his left hand traced along the pale skin of his thigh to where the bullet was lodged. "I . . . I can't do it. . . ."

"Terrapin. I want to know about Terrapin."

"He was there," Pinder said desperately, "at Crowheart. After . . . after Cole Malone got bushwhacked, Terrapin put me in charge."

"How many of you are there?"

"We done split up into three groups. The others went east, maybe up into the Big Horns. But . . . Terrapin made me do it . . . said he'd kill—"

"You're a filthy liar, Pinder!" Marshal Philby lashed out. "You rustle cattle and kill of your own free will. What were you to do with the stolen cattle?"

"Head them up toward Sheridan along with Terrapin's herd."

Taking a backward step, Philby said, "You heard him." And bending toward the outlaw, he added, "I'll take my knife now."

"What about this here slug?"

Fishing out a cigar, Marshal Philby bit the tip away. "There's some hanging trees along the river."

"No!" Ike Pinder screamed, and before anyone realized his intention he brought the knife up and plunged it into his heart. His accusing eyes went to Philby's face before they became fixed in death.

A half-hour later four pairs of worn boots were touching air along the Big Horn river as those who'd hung the rustlers went to see about the cattle. While out on the open prairie Ike Pinder and the other dead rustlers were awaiting the coming of dawn and the vultures.

"Men such as that," Marshal Philby said gravely, "deserve no Christian burial. Well, Mr. Byrum, you others, I'll need you to testify against Terrapin if we ever get him into a court of law. And again, much obliged."

"Marshal, it troubles me some leaving those rustlers like that," said the rancher. "I'll leave the ones we hanged dancing in the wind for a spell. For the others, a shallow grave will do."

"Sympathy has killed many a man."

"This is practicality, Marshal. Just don't want to get caught upwind of any bloated carcasses."

19

One day seemed to blend into another for the Rocking K hands working cattle out of the breaks along the Sweetwater River. Well before sunup would see them in the saddle astride cutting horses, which they'd change for others while nooning, and then it was back into the thickets and thorny brush and twisting arroyos in their search for cattle. Daily, too, the herd being tended farther north on the flats was growing larger, the days searing hot as summer came fully upon the Shoshone Basin.

As was their custom, the men carried sidearms and rifles, while Jake Woodley wore the harried look of a man sensing his past was about to come a-calling. Woodley couldn't shake the notion he was being watched. Nor the sight of that girl he'd gunned down back at Rock Springs.

"Though that lousy sheriff deserved to be backshot," he muttered as he ran a gloved finger under his sweat-drenched shirt collar.

"Could sure use some rotgut," the man beside him said.

"Well, there ain't any," Woodley said sourly.

"Didn't mean to rouse your dander any."

"I'll tell you what, Morgan, working for the Rocking K is gettin' to me. That Etta's plain hell on wheels."

"Terrapin ain't much better."

"The question is, how long can they keep up this rustling?"

"These here ain't rustled cattle, Woodley."

"I'm speakin' of the stuff Cole Malone's bunch brings down here. There's been talk of a ranch war."

"So what?"

"I was a bluebelly, Morgan. Seen my share of killin' at Vicksburg and Shiloh."

"How come this sudden spate of conscience?"

"Jawin' with you ain't gettin' me no place." They reached the lip of an arroyo. "Let's get to work."

Woodley watched the other hand ride east along the arroyo before he urged his horse down a sloping break in the clayey wall and through clutching underbrush.

Shaking out his lariat to form a small loop, his eyes flicked to the peaks – the Rattlesnakes to the north, the Greens opposite – both ranges flowing almost dead east. Beyond them lay the Laramies stretching due south. What was to stop him, he mused, from just keeping on riding thataway. He was getting lamed to the saddle, just another hardcase whose time was running out. Nobody gave a damn, either. A sobering fact that had been gnawing at his thoughts and changing his opinion of himself, of the men he rode with. Back at Rock Springs his finger had eagerly pulled the trigger to kill that sheriff. Then that girl had gone down.

Once upon a time in his prideful days, there'd been another dark-haired girl like that, with him in his Yankee uniform a-courting her. Before leaving for the fighting again a date had been set for their wedding. And then, down near a place called Shiloh in Tennessee a letter bearing strange handwriting had been placed in his hand by a mail clerk. A Sunday morning, he would forever after recall, the smell of frying bacon and boiling coffee coming to him, along with the dreaded Reb yell as the Confederates had struck from the woods; and, the letter shoved into a blouse pocket and forgotten, he'd found himself fighting to stay alive. A rejoicing Jake Woodley had been one of the victorious survivors, and only when reading the letter did he wish otherwise, for it told of his betrothed succumbing to smallpox. At that moment his heart had withered and died. Stayed that way all of these bloody and useless years. What he felt now was shame, remorse, the need to get away.

The blow when it came to the back of Jake Woodley's head brought no outcry, and before his limp form toppled out of the saddle, Jed Starlight was there. Grabbing the reins before Woodley's horse could bolt away, he held the man draped across his saddle while heading back into underbrush to his ground-hitched horse. Quickly he used the hardcases lariat to lash him astride his horse.

Going onto four days now Starlight had been tracking Jake Woodley, ever since he'd come across those peculiar star markings left by Woodley's boots back along an arm of the Sweetwater. This was the man who'd done harm to Crystal Lane. Strong in Jed was the temptation to cut Woodley's throat from corner to corner, and lift his scalplock. But Starlight hadn't come to the point where he could kill a helpless man. He needed Woodley alive, to clear his name, wanted to see him stretch hemp the legal way.

Lithely Starlight regained his saddle, though in doing so a slight tinge of pain came from the side wound. His plan was to work around the Rocking K cowpunchers, gathering their herd and somehow make his way to the ranch, there to force a showdown with Etta Montclair Lane—and Terrapin, if he was there. By now, he figured, Keno Lane should have gotten back.

Coming out onto the arroyo bottom, Jed rode loping to the west until this break in the land started rising toward the plains, and he went onto them, only to find to his dismay that four hardcases were cantering less than a mile away. Upon espying Starlight, they spurred their mounts into a gallop and reached for their handguns.

Wheeling his bronc around, and the other horse, Jed pounded down into the arroyo and sped along its narrow bottom to where it suddenly widened and revealed another Rocking K hand hazing some steers Jed's way. Both men went for their revolvers, with Jed's barking first, again, and the man blocking his eastward progress toppled backward out of his saddle. Without breaking stride he was past the scattering cattle and riderless horse. A backward glance showed him the other hardcases coming hard, and Starlight's lashing reins brought the bronc stretching out more.

Out on the plains sloping toward the foothills went Starlight. Here there wasn't much shelter, just mesquite and sagebrush, and to the unwary horseman, holes made by burrowing animals. Jed ignored this danger as the distance began to widen, the horses of those chasing him slackening off as they tired. Once in a while a shot fanned air or dusted the ground well behind Starlight. Suddenly the hardcases gave up, but Jed let his bronc go full-out until a dip in the terrain carried him out of their view. Slowing to a canter, he then began to swing southward toward the Sweetwater shining under a late afternoon sun.

After the horses had caught their wind, and had drunk sparingly, Starlight veered away from the river to work his way at a walk toward the eastern fringes of the Rattlesnakes, and to the stirring groans of Jake Woodley. Jed's presence stirred up some pronghorns, and dancing off a ways, the curious animals swung around to study this intruder. They were still within rifle range, but he had other game in mind.

Camp for Jed Starlight was up on a rocky ledge with an overhang and a clear view of where he'd just ridden. He was none too gentle with the hardcase when he unlashed him from atop his horse, letting Woodley drop heavily to the stony ground, and the man cried out, "That hurt, dammit." But he was still groggy and made little attempt to fight as Starlight pinioned the rope around his arms and legs and left him perched with his back against a boulder.

"You're that kid . . . Starlight?"

Swearing didn't come natural to Starlight, but there was a need for it now. "And you're the sonofabitch who shot Crystal!"

"It wasn't done a-purpose . . . I swear, kid."

"Did Terrapin order it done?"

"It was you I was after. But, yeah, Terrapin's behind this. And so's that bitch, Etta."

"You telling me this to save your skin?"

180

"I'm telling you this, kid, 'cause I had it in mind to clear the hell out of this territory. That gal goin' down . . . it done brought back too many painful memories."

"How does Keno Lane fit in all of this?" said Starlight as he traded his boots for the moccasins.

"He don't. All these years Keno's been suckered by that bitch of an Etta. You know, kid, there's somethin' about you. It makes me think right of off Keno?"

"Once upon a time, or so the story goes, I was called Jed Lane," Starlight said pensively.

A glimmer of understanding flashed in Woodley's eyes. "Now it begins to make sense." But he'd spoken to himself, for Starlight had slipped away into the gathering darkness.

When Jed returned, nearly an hour later, he was carrying a rabbit draped over one shoulder and an armful of buffer chips. Wordlessly he used the buffer chips to make a smokeless fire under the overhang. Then he skinned his catch, and put it on a stick over the flames supported by a couple of rocks. As it roasted, Jed sat on his haunches with his hat tugged low; under it, his eyes checked out the distant stretch of basin. Once in a while the hardcase would tug at the ropes binding him, but he didn't complain or try to engage the kid in conversation. Nor did he anticipate sharing in the kid's meal or having his thirst slaked, since he saw no coffee pot heating over the low flames.

After a while curiosity caused Woodley to say, "I've got a pretty good notion of why you nabbed me, kid. Besides the girl, I'm the only one who knows what happened back there at Rock Springs. Just hope she's still alive."

"Why's that?" Jed said cuttingly.

"A man ain't a man what makes war on women. Had

181

a gal once like that myself. Back East, it was. Only she up and passed away on me. That's what done me in, I reckon."

Starlight turned his eyes upon the hardcase. He saw hard, cynical eyes in a face stubbled by beard and seared by wind, the scurvy clothing of a man used to hard times, the soles of the man's boots, a hole in one and those star markings on both run-down heels. But there hadn't been any sarcasm in Jake Woodley's voice, the words spoken had been filled with regret, and maybe despair. The hardcases thieving days were over and he knew it.

"They'll hang you once I bring you back."

"Know that," came the indifferent response.

"What's your handle?"

"Jake Woodley."

"What will your testimony be, Jake Woodley?"

"To you, kid, it's that I'm tired of what I've become. I'm plumb worn out, body and soul. Heard a preacher speak once of every man having a spirit. Mine's sure fled this body a long time ago. To them what jails me I'll just be the killer of that sheriff."

Gazing somberly at the flames, Jed said, "Hanging ain't a pretty sight."

"Kid, it's just come to me that I've been dead all these years. Ever since the woman I was to marry up and died. Hanging'll be something to enjoy, for me, that is."

Jed sliced a hunk of rabbit away, then picking up his canteen, he strode over to the hardcase, whose eyes flared open in surprise. "Can't untie you," said Jed, as he uncorked the canteen and held it so the man could drink.

After he'd drunk his full, Woodley said, "Obliged —

and don't blame you none for not untying me."

After, Jed held the piece of meat so that Woodley's teeth clamped on it. Then he padded back to the fire to hunker down and eat his own supper while thinking of what was to come, back at the Rocking K ranch when he rode in with his prisoner, and afterward.

20

Keno Lane brought his buggy along the prairie-gouged road to where it took a sharp turn toward the Sweetwater. The road had deep wheel ruts and a grassy center that brushed against the undercarriage, the buggy wheels sinking into the muddy bank sloping riverward. To water splashing and iron-rimmed wheels clanging on an occasional rock, he forded to come up the northern bank and back onto prairie. Darby Lane, astride Keno's horse, a rangy grulla, had gone on ahead, but now he returned and fell in alongside the buggy. Though the yonker didn't carry a sidearm, in his saddle boot was Keno's "Yellow Boy," the old brassy-green Henry rifle Lane had used back when he was scouting for the army.

Their departure from Rock Springs had been delayed because of Crystal's condition, and during that time Keno had gone in search of the U.S. marshal only to learn that Ezra Philby had trailed out. He'd wanted to tell the marshal that Jedekiah Starlight wasn't any horse thief or murderer. Those shocking words of Crystal's—that Starlight could be his own flesh and blood—still rang clear in Keno's thoughts. But he was afraid to confront the past, fearing that Jed Starlight would't prove out. However, there was that birthmark! Along with Crystal's firm belief that he was indeed Jed Lane.

While back in Rock Springs Keno Lane had visited the rooms of Amanda Delaplaine, a middle-aged woman of considerable beauty. In Keno's scouting days she'd been the young wife of an army officer, Lee Delaplaine, destined to become a colonel and die in the Indian Wars. Only when she had begun to support Keno's campaign had he learned of her inherited wealth.

"Evening, Mrs. Delaplaine." Doffing his hat, Keno stepped over the threshold and eased the door shut.

"You know me better than that, Keno."

"Sorry, Amanda."

"How is Crystal?"

"Coming along," he said quietly, exchanging his hat for a glass of sherry. Amanda placed it on a table as they crossed to a divan.

"Political campaigns are never easy," she said.

"It's more than that, I'm afraid . . . more than Crystal getting hurt, too." As she settled down on the divan, he caught a glimpse of creamy-skinned bosom pressing against the silky green dress. She had hazel eyes, light brown hair coiffing an oval face, and full lips dusted with a touch of red lipstick. Keno had strong feelings for her, more than a married man should. That troubled him. He wasn't all that much of a Puritan, having in the past done some straying, mostly with women who hung out at dance halls or saloons. When Etta had simply cut herself off from him, the ranch becoming her master, Keno Lane had become more hired hand than husband. He'd learned to live with it. But the presence of Amanda Delaplaine in his life these past few months had brought a new awareness of himself, along with a virile strut to his walk. She was vibrant, alive—had an ability to draw him out—and she would grace any ballroom or social gathering, unlike the forced presence, or so it seemed, of Etta.

Without realizing it Keno downed the sherry, in his eyes the unfocused glaze of a man deep in thought, and he felt more than saw Amanda rise and take his glass, to go over and refill it and come back to his side. "Oh, thanks, I . . ."

"Care to talk about it?"

"Reckon I would, Amanda. My son's alive, or so I'm told."

"Wasn't he taken by Indians?"

"So the story was told to me. By my wife." Keno's voice crackled with bitterness.

Easing down, but at the other end of the divan, their knees almost touching, Amanda Delaplaine resisted the temptation to reach for his hand. She'd fallen in love with Keno; it was as simple as that. But she would never tell him, or insist upon receiving any special favors for all the money she'd given to his campaign. There was a sad melancholy air about him. If he could only be as I once knew him, she mused, that dashing army scout, sure in his knowledge of the

Indian and of the trackless waste that was Territorial Wyoming, and of his prowess over women. Even then, back at Fort Laramie, she'd been attracted to him, though Keno Lane had paid no more attention to her than he had to the other officers' wives.

"I have no choice, Amanda, but to withdraw from the campaign."

"Keno, you mustn't."

"No other option is open to me. All of these years"—harshly the words came out of Keno Lane—"I never really knew my wife. That she could be capable of ordering my son killed . . ." A bitter sigh came from Keno as he leaned back against the cushions. "Would you believe that before Etta married me she was an outlaw. Sister to Cole Malone. Both of them used my ranch to receive stolen cattle."

Easing toward him, Amanda said, "This seems so . . . unreal."

"Their first step was to get rid of my son so hers could take over the ranch after I'm gone. A wonder she just didn't up and kill me a long time ago."

"Can you prove this?"

"I found this out from Crystal. At first I put it down to ravings caused by what had happened to her. Can't be true! I told myself. But then my brain knew . . . and this chilling feeling came over me, as if a rabbit was running over my grave. My *segundo*, Terrapin, bungled the job when he took my son out Wind River way. Left him staked out so wild critters could find him. Seems some mountain man came along to save my son, raise him. But Terrapin did this on Etta's orders."

"What are you going to do, Keno?"

"For certain I'm out of politics. Already spoken to

187

my campaign manager about that. Soon's Crystal can travel, we're trailing back to the Rocking K."

"Going back there could be dangerous. Couldn't you just turn this over to the law?"

"I figured it's time, Amanda, to measure up to what I was before."

"When will you be leaving?"

"At first light, I'm a-hoping."

Standing up, Amanda held out her hand and said, "Come."

Questioningly Keno Lane rose.

"I want you to stay here tonight."

A hawk soaring into Keno's line of vision brought him back onto prairie again. They'd rolled onto Rocking K land. Wistfully his eyes went to the immense tract he owned; he had no feeling of pride. Some of this land had been gained through crooked means. Once he'd confronted Etta, and dealt with Terrapin, it was Keno's intention to sell off chunks of his ranch in an attempt to square things with the other ranchers in the basin. He could be facing a few years in prison, and he deserved them, he thought, for trusting his wife.

At South Pass City, Keno had learned of Jed Starlight's jailbreak, and that U.S. Marshal Philby and his men had passed through. From an old acquaintance Keno had also found out about Terrapin's hiring some hardcases and then heading out for parts unknown. Perhaps into the mountains where they'd hook up with the Cole Malone gang. Once matters had been squared away at the ranch, Keno Lane would begin searching for his son.

"Crystal, I just hope that Jed is holed up some-place." His soft whistle brought the pair of horses into a ground-eating canter.

"I've a feeling he is, Keno."

"He seems to have made quite an impression on you."

Her face crimsoning, Crystal leaned over and placed her hand on Keno's shirt sleeve. "He's so like you. Only lately have I begun to realize just how lonely you've been all of these years."

"Done some soul-searching myself, gal. Guess I've kept my distance from you and Darby."

"I don't want it that way anymore, Keno."

"Trouble is, I'm calling it quits with Etta. Gal, I'm sure sorry for not getting to know you more . . . you and Darby."

"I hope all Etta gets is a prison sentence."

"What she deserves, I reckon. Though there's a chance she could hang."

Nodding sadly, Crystal said, "Jed really isn't my brother."

"I suppose not. Why?"

"Because I've fallen in love with him."

"That sure shakes the squirrels out of the trees. Does he know how you feel?"

"Nope."

"Gonna tell him?"

"Yup."

They smiled at one another, sharing a tender moment of closeness, and then Darby Lane shouted out that he'd spotted the ranch buildings. Keno brought the buggy on to where he had a clear view of the ranch site. Except for the smitty working at the open-walled blacksmith shop and a few horses idling in the pole corrals, the place seemed deserted. Inside the main house would be the two Mex cooks and the other servants, and also his wife. Distantly, about a mile to the northeast, the cattle being tended by about a half-dozen cowpunchers were grazing over several hundred yards of prairie. "I tally around four hundred head," Keno murmured silently as he pulled out his .45 Peacemaker and spun the cylinder to check the loads in it. He was edgy, sensing that Terrapin was nearby and in the showdown to come he could be a-breathing his last. The thought sobered him, and steeling his mind for what was to come, Keno waved Darby over to the buggy.

"Son, you know the situation. When we get down there, I'll ease the buggy over to the bunkhouse. You and Crystal stay in there until I clear this whole mess up."

"You gonna gun down my ma?"

"Think I should?"

"She done wrong," he said firmly.

"Though she deserves it," Keno said painfully, "nope. And, Darby, make sure you take old Yellow Boy along in case things get out of hand."

They set out across the lowering floor of the plains toward the scattering of buildings located just north of the Sweetwater, the wind picking up more as it swept hotly out of the southwest. They were unaware of being glassed by U.S. Marshal Ezra Philby from a distant elevation.

Lowering the field glass, Philby commented dryly, "Appears to be Keno Lane. And riding into a trap."

"How'd you figure that, Ezra?"

"Cowpunchers generally don't take afternoon naps in pole barns, not three of them. Saw Terrapin's glass eye a-winking in the sun too."

"It makes no sense them gunning down Keno?"

"A woman such as Etta Lane's got no common sense," Philby said laconically, as he dragged in cigar smoke. "She's tetched, boys, crazy for money and power. Which means we'd best head out. No telling what that woman will do when Keno braces her. It's a good two-hour ride down there. Could be we'll be too late." He spurred his mount along the high mesa.

21

His tension building, Keno Lane brought the buggy in at a slow lope along the dirt road, to where it spread out more before passing through a wide gateway. Something just doesn't feel right, he mused tautly, while taking in the front door of the rambling fieldstone main house. It stood open, the curtains fluttering behind open windows, and he heard the ringing of a hammer as the smitty pounded a red-hot shoe into shape. Keno's hand sought the holstered gun, let go of the pearl-inlaid butt when one of the Mex cooks appeared behind the house but didn't glance around while going to the outhouse.

Flicking a finger against his Stetson at the smitty's casual wave, Keno swept past an oak tree and found the screening wall of the bunkhouse. He sat there holding the reins as Darby helped his sister out of the buggy seat; then, gripping Darby's shoulder, Keno said tersely, "Remember, stay put." A quick smile tugged at his lips. "Just for the record, I love you kids."

He clucked his team into motion, only to have a cold chill rattle down his spine when he discovered that the smitty had left the blacksmith shop. But without slowing down, he went over to pull up in front of the main house, and in dismounting, he studied the lay of the other buildings, knowing he'd ridden into a trap — one that wouldn't have been laid by Etta. She needed him. Hell, she was going to be the first lady of the Grand State of Wyoming. Hadn't she rustled cattle all these years, probably done killing so she could have her name etched in history when he became governor. So, he reckoned, there'd been a falling out with Terrapin, who was there someplace. The man's stalking presence came strong to Keno, brought back memories of times when it was either him or a Cree or Sioux.

Tying up at the hitching rack, he moved warily along the pathway fringed with flowers and shrubbery. Many a time he'd come staggering up this stony path after a week's drunk to find Etta off someplace and he'd had to sober up alone while fighting the ghosts of the past. Pondering on it, had he ever loved the woman? She'd been a saucy tart, had been Etta Montclair Lane, lusting for him early on and then drying up like the land after a season or two of drought.

Keno stopped just short of the stone steps running up to the front porch with the wide overhanging roof and the iron railing. When he made out the shadowy figure of his wife standing inside the doorway, he said bitterly, "You know why I'm here, damn you! First you get rid of my son! Then you try to poison your daughter! Damn, woman, you've got no soul!"

"That was Terrapin's idea," she said savagely, and now Keno Lane became aware of the rifle Etta was holding, but she still stood in shadow as if that would shield her from the truth of what was to come.

In a voice pitched with anguish Keno said, "You're

lying! You've used me . . . destroyed my name! Damn you, Etta, you was an outlaw when I married you. And you're still in that thievin' game."

A finger crooked in the trigger guard, the other bony hand cupped under the rifle stock, Etta stepped into sunlight, and Keno was visibly shaken by her haggard appearance. The oncoming wind tumbled her uncombed hair around her bare shoulders, but there was defiance in Etta's crazed eyes as she said vehemently, "Clear your mind, Keno. All these years I was building up this place while you were out whoring around. You fool, you can still win the election."

"Etta," Keno said sorrowfully, "you're plumb loco. It's over, woman."

"I'll tell you when it's over," she shrieked, and Keno recoiled from the sight of her lips curling back, teeth fanging out; knowing he was but a hair's-breadth from being gutshot. Somehow he forced a smile. "Etta, you were never much of a shot."

"But I am, Keno!"

Just then, Terrapin eased around the corner of the house, and the hardcase motioned with his drawn gun for Keno to lift his arms. Then he said cuttingly, "You damned fool, you've had blinders on for years. Full of self-pity. And sometimes so damned liquored up you didn't know an ace from a deuce. Or who you slept with last."

Gripped with anger, all Keno Lane could do was stand there and take abuse from the man who'd done away with his son. Terrapin's low monotone went on cutting into him, opening all of those old wounds, trying to goad him into going for his .45 Peacemaker, a weapon he hadn't fired in years.

Clicking the hammer back, Terrapin glanced toward the porch at Etta Lane. "You gonna do it or me?"

"It doesn't have to be this way."

194

Malicious laughter seemed to dance in Terrapin's glass eye. "Etta, no way good old Keno here is gonna stay alive so's he can testify against us. Hell, woman, you knew that back at Rock Springs. For that same reason you tried to poison Crystal. Well, Mrs. Lane?"

As Etta reached back to work the lever, her eyes went wavering past Keno, widened suddenly in fear and disbelief, and then Terrapin saw the horsemen, one bound to his saddle, the other, the kid Starlight, sighting down his rifle barrel, and Etta screamed, "It's . . . Jed!"

Ignoring the guns leveled at him, Keno spun around to let his questing eyes take in Starlight, and right off, no longer doubting, he knew it was his son. He also glimpsed, out of the corner of his eye, movement over by the pole corral; then three men he knew to be Rocking K hands came out warily. Now Keno's only concern was for his son being caught in a crossfire. But Jed Starlight's words took the play away from the rancher.

"Drop your gun, Terrapin!" Starlight ordered.

"Reckon not, kid," he said derisively. " 'Cause my boys have got you covered."

Just as Starlight spotted the other hardcases, flame spouted from Terrapin's six-gun. Only it was Etta Lane who felt the slug pierce her body. As she stumbled backward mortally wounded, the heavy report of Starlight's rifle answered the guns of the hardcases, and then Terrapin ducked around the south wall of the house.

His spurs chinking on the stone steps, Keno hurried to his wife's side. He knelt down and cradled her in his arms. The waxy contours of Etta's face told Keno everything, as did her gasping words, "Governor, Keno . . . you could have been . . ." Blood trickled out of her mouth when she spoke, then her head turned limply to

195

rest upon his arm. And when Keno lowered her down he was almost certain that in the exchange of gunfire a gun had sounded back of the house.

But the rancher's immediate concern was to help Jed Starlight. He picked up Etta's rifle, sighted at one of the hardcases crouched near the blacksmith shop only to have the hammer strike an empty breech. Levering the rifle, he discovered it didn't contain any shells. Somehow, he concluded, Terrapin had emptied Etta's rifle, and his contempt for the man grew.

The next moment Starlight was there, flinging himself out of the saddle, while bullets were ricocheting off the porch and house walls. Tossing the rifle aside, Keno unleathered his Peacemaker and gave him some covering fire as Starlight cut the thongs binding his prisoner, then all three men sought the house, on the way a bullet nicking Keno's arm and drawing blood.

One of servants appeared to say, "Señor Lane, your son Darby, he has killed Terrapin!"

"Darby? If that don't beat all. Where's Crystal?"

"The *señorita* is here, in the *cocina.*"

Keno ignored his wound as he stepped to a window to brush a curtain aside. He saw that one of the hardcases was riding bareback toward the herd ground. And Keno swung around to say, "I may own this spread, but Etta's sure enough paid for the loyalty of the hands. Gents, we've got ourselves some trouble." Holstering his revolver, he gave the next few moments to his son.

There was this fierce longing in Keno Lane to embrace Jed, but the years of going it almost alone, of keeping his emotions shielded, held him rooted to the hardwood floor. Finally, his voice breaking, Keno said, "Jed, how I've missed you."

"Guess you're my . . . father," Starlight said guardedly. He jabbed a thumb toward Jake Woodley, who was still rubbing his wrists to get the circulation back into them. "Another Rocking K hand."

"It was me, Mr. Lane, who bushwhacked that sheriff over to Rock Springs. Mostly, though, I regret your daughter gettin' hurt."

"*Señors,* they come!" announced one of the Mex servants. "Many *caballos!*"

Thereupon the voice of Darby Lane preceded him into the living room, "Count me in." Though his face was drawn, in his hands he grasped Keno's Henry rifle.

Blinking his surprise away, Keno said, "Tell us about Terrapin?"

"I seen Jed there a-coming in. Along with spotting them men hiding out in that pole barn. Right off, I figured you might need some help. I . . . I saw Terrapin first . . . holding his gun. Knew he would try to harm us, Keno, so I just up and fired old Yellow Boy here; downed him the first shot."

"For certain you've got grit, Darby. Well, men, pick a window which pleases you. But hold your fire until we know their intentions."

"Maybe I could go out and palaver with them," ventured Woodley, which brought everyone's eyes to him. "Once they find out Etta and Terrapin are dead, well, could be there won't be no gunplay."

"Any objections, Jed?"

He glanced at Keno, then back at the hardcase. "Can't give you no gun, Woodley."

"Didn't ask for none."

"Go to it, then."

"Obliged to you for trusting me, kid." Stepping to the open doorway, he forced a tentative smile and tugged at his hat while moving outside.

Crouched at a window, his rifle resting on the sill, Starlight gazed beyond Jake Woodley who was striding out into the yard, to the Rocking K hands, who

197

were dismounting hurriedly and unsheathing their rifles before finding shelter. They'd all been involved in one type of unlawful activity or another, with most of them having down some rustling for the Rocking K. This was the reason, mused Starlight, they couldn't leave any witnesses behind. He stared back at Woodley, who was doffing his hat and waving it, and shouting, "Terrapin, Etta Lane, they've cashed in their chips. Keno's running the place. Wants to talk to you men."

"Time for jawing is past, Woodley!"

"That you, Milburn?"

The sharp crackle of the hardcase's rifle cut Woodley off in midsentence, and he grunted in pain and doubled up before flopping to the dusty ground. The same rifle turned its killing intensity upon the ranch house, and the others opened fire; spraying at the windows and doors. They kept it up for several minutes without receiving any return fire.

"What do you think, Jed?"

"We've got troubles for certain. How's this place fixed for ammo?"

"Got enough of that. But come nightfall, I'm afraid they'll try to burn us out. Won't rush us until then. Got to admire Woodley for what he did."

"He was a-cravin' to die," commented Jed.

"You know, boys" — Keno smiled — "I've got this powerful urge for some hot java . . . and some Mex chow." He yelled toward the kitchen. "*Pedro, tengo hambre. Tortillas, café.*"

Darby, who'd been keeping watch at a window opening onto the northwest, spun away from it and yelled, "Riders coming in!"

Starlight and Keno moved over, with Keno exclaiming, "One of them is wearing a suit."

Starlight muttered: "It's that U.S. marshal. Let's give him and his men some covering fire." But when he hurried to station himself at another window, it was to find most of the hardcases heading for their saddled mounts, and he emptied his rifle at them, then pulled out his handgun, only to have them ride out of range.

He trailed Keno and Darby out the front door, past the body of Etta Lane; and spreading out, they added their covering fire to that of the lawmen, Keno saying, "Now we've got them caught in a crossfire."

A mutter of pain from Jake Woodley, who was sprawled out in the yard, brought Starlight over to him in a crouch. Jed triggered lead at the hardcases shielded by an oak tree, then looked at Woodley to determine the extent of his wound.

"High in the right shoulder," Woodley grimaced. "Figured it best to play possum until this was over. I still aim to tell the truth of it back at Rock Springs."

The lawmen swept in between buildings and the corrals, driving before them those hardcases who hadn't been able to get away, and now the sound of gunfire began to die out. Closing to where Jed was hunkered by the hardcase, Keno opened the cylinder on his Peacemaker and emptied it of shells, and when Philby rode up to him, he tossed the gun to the marshal.

"Obliged for your help."

"My job," intoned Marshal Philby. "I'll be a-taking you in, Keno."

"Expected that."

Philby stared at the body of Etta Lane and said, "How about Terrapin?"

"He's dead, too," Keno said pensively. Wistfully he gazed at his two sons. At least, he thought bitterly, I have Jed back. He didn't look forward to the prospect of a jail sentence, or if it came to that, his hanging, but it had to be that way, for too many good men had gone under because of his wife and her outlaw brother.

"You'll be wanting to bury your wife, Keno. We'll take time for that, and for burying some of the others. Know a heap about you, Keno Lane. Meaning a lot of folks in these parts think you aren't mixed up in what was going on out here. That's up to the federal judge, though."

"It's enough for me, Marshal Philby, that my son is back. What more can a man want?"

"Reckon so, Keno, reckon so."

22

Freedom was a golden eagle winging ahead of Jed Starlight, the wind carrying down the scent of pine from mountainous heights being caressed by dusking shards of sunlight, the Wind River a westward beacon, and civilization left behind two days ago. Freedom. His head felt clearer as Starlight's senses awakened to the life he loved, though part of that love had been given to Crystal Lane who was riding alongside him. Because of her presence, Jed hadn't given the high sign to the settlements of the Great Plains as had been Cree Bonner's custom.

Freedom.

Back at the Rocking K Ranch, a sort of restrained liberty had been ceded to Keno Lane, the result of his trial over at Lander. Except for some breeding stock, at Keno's insistence, the Rocking K herd already gathered had been driven to Sheridan and sold to a cattle buyer. Keno had distributed the money it brought to basin ranchers, and he'd disposed of some land, too. It had been a humbling experience for Keno, this being placed on probation, but chiefly a time, in these dying months of summer, when he'd gotten acquainted with his son, Jed.

"You're right, son," Keno had said, "about a man listening to the dictates of his heart."

"Crystal feels the same way."

"So you're set on marrying her?"

"Figure on doing that while passing through Arapahoe."

"Mountain living?" Keno said pensively. "Can be rough."

"Tougher down here at times."

"You'll be back, I expect."

"Yup, pa, I'll be back."

He could still feel Keno's large arms closing to embrace him, the gleam of pain in his father's eyes; but Jed Starlight knew his destiny lay at timberline. During his absence, Jed figured, Keno and the yonker Darby would carve out a future for the Rocking K. He'd miss them for sure, and so would Crystal.

Starlight's excitement over where they were heading got to the horses they rode, and to the pack horse, and they kept stepping up to run and prancing sideways; but with night closing fast he and Crystal kept them reined in. She cast sidelong glances at land she'd never seen before, at the narrowing red walls closing around them, the river glinting under a cloudless sky.

Mystically, and to Starlight's unrestrained joy, stars began poking holes in the blackening sky, the wind hushing now as a monstrous harvest moon lipped the eastern horizon to pour out orange moonlight. Now they rode as if by day, shedding their fears of what night would bring.

"It was on such a night as this Cree Bonner found me."

"Along this very river, you told me. Doesn't it bother

202

you coming back here?"

"All my ghosts are laid to rest, Crystal."

The river crooked around huge rocks serrated by eons of water erosion and weather, and they came upon aspens shimmering over a grassy meadow. Veering that way, Starlight and his woman slipped from their saddles. Once again the silvery cast of starlight found his face, showing to his woman and this night that Jed's quest was over.

HIGH-TECH WARRIORS IN A
DEVASTATED FUTURE!
C.A.D.S.
BY JOHN SIEVERT

#1: C.A.D.S. (1641, $3.50)

Wearing seven-foot high Computerized Attack/Defense System suits equipped with machine guns, armor-piercing shells and flame throwers, Colonel Dean Sturgis and the men of C.A.D.S. are America's last line of defense after the East Coast of the U.S. is shattered by a deadly Soviet nuclear first strike!

#2: TECH BATTLEGROUND (1790, $2.95)

At the secret American base at White Sands, New Mexico, the President gives the order for a suicide raid on Charlotte, North Carolina—command HQ for the Soviet invaders and anchor point for half the Red fleet. Colonel Dean Sturgis and his C.A.D.S. force suit up for action in a deadly assault where the odds for success are a thousand to one!

#3: TECH COMMANDO (1893, $2.95)

The fate of America hangs in the balance as the men of C.A.D.S. battle to prevent the Russians from expanding their toehold in the U.S. For Colonel Dean Sturgis it means destroying the key link in the main Sov military route—the heavily defended Chesapeake Bay Bridge-Tunnel!

#4: TECH STRIKE FORCE (1993, $2.95)

An American turncoat is about to betray the C.A.D.S. ultra-sensitive techno-secrets to the Reds. The arch traitor and his laser-equipped army of renegades must be found and smashed, and the men of C.A.D.S. will accomplish the brutal task—or die trying!

#5: TECH SATAN (2313, $2.95)

The new U.S. government at White Sands, New Mexico suddenly goes off the air and the expeditionary C.A.D.S. force must find out why. But the soldiers of tomorrow find their weapons useless against a killer plague that threatens to lay bare to the Soviet invaders the last remaining bastion of American freedom!